Bread and Roses
Book 2

The Duke's Perfect Wife

REBECCAH WILSON

Dedication

For my dad, who lit my spark of interest in writing.
I miss you immeasurably.

Acknowledgements

From the bottom of my heart, I want to thank everyone who supported me throughout the process of getting this story out into the world. To my family and community, who kept me going when I wanted to give up, and forgave my sudden disappearances when inspiration struck, I so appreciate it. You all are my rock. It wasn't easy, and still you jumped up to lend a hand—or an ear. And of course, thank you to my intrepid editor, Eugenia, who helped guide me through the wilderness to find the story I was trying to tell. I really couldn't have done it without you.

Chapter

One

Buckinghamshire, England
September 1893

Mena fought back a wave of anger as she faced down her disapproving father. This was no small feat, especially for a woman who had been raised to acquiesce to every whim of her parents. Thankfully her mother was gone and could no longer reach Mena with her sharp words and pointed barbs. Nor could she deny Mena food, as she often had done. Mena's stomach grumbled at the distant memory of the endless hunger that had filled so many of her days.

"I am simply not going, and that is final," she stated in a steady voice that belied her discomfort.

Sir Harvey-Morton was a rotund man with impressive jowls and whimsical puffs of white hair adorning his balding head. His ruddy cheeks shook as he frowned. Noting the glint of censure in her father's eyes, Mena squared her shoulders for the fight that was to ensue. She could tell when he wanted something, and it put her on high alert.

"We were both invited, and I can hardly go by myself," Sir Harvey-Morton pointed out, crossing his meaty arms over his belly.

"Why not?" she asked innocently, knowing full well how ridiculous it would be for her father to attend a weekend party at the duke's estate on his own—an aging man among young ladies prowling for a husband.

"You know why not. And besides, it will do you good to be there. You need to get out more," he said with a smug grin Mena rolled her eyes and turned away, feigning interest in the books that lined the shelf along the wall beside her. She picked up a slim volume and thumbed through it, studiously ignoring her father. She hated when he thought he was being clever.

But the man would not quit that easily. He took the book from her hands and closed it, replacing it on the shelf. Then he took Mena by the arms and turned her to face him.

"My dear girl, you know that I only want what is best for you," he began, and Mena sighed. "Your mother's dying wish was to see you settled in a good marriage, to a man of means. And since you are not even attempting to find one of those, and I am not forcing you to do so, could you just indulge me a bit and rub elbows with the elite for a few days?" he wheedled.

Mena stared into her father's blue eyes, still bright and boyish despite his years. He had always been her ally, even when the finishing school selected by her mother had sent her back (and refused a refund). He had not pushed. He had allowed her to spend her days as she wished, watching her slide comfortably into spinsterhood with nary a complaint.

Was it really too much of him to ask her to spend a few days enjoying the comforts of a duke's fancy country seat? Surely, she would survive a picnic or two, and some parlor games. After all, Mena had plenty of practice pretending to be a conventional woman with suitable interests before. She had a lifetime of experience playing the part. What was one more weekend?

Long buried memories bubbled up. Ferocious young girls sniping with their words, pinching hands pulling laces tight enough to suffocate, meals consisting of only thin broths and fruit.

"Think of it as acting," Ashley had once told her.

Her old friend's voice, hushed and bitter, echoed in Mena's memory. As the children of aspirational parents, they had both been sent to one of the best finishing schools in England. Ashley's parents were country gentry from a town in the north of England and had their sights set on an aristocratic husband for their only daughter. Through her they planned to dip their grasping hands into the coffers of some high-born family, but alas, for them it was not to be. Ashley was not destined to marry a lord after all, and had instead escaped to pursue a very different, and much more honest existence far away from their influence. Mena was immensely proud of her dear friend, but she missed her too.

So, Mena would play the part of dutiful daughter once again. This time though, at the advanced age of twenty-seven, and with her mother long gone, Mena could write her own script. She was free of the woman's control.

Her lips quirked up in a smile.

"Alright father, but I won't stand for any manipulations. I am going on my own terms. Only I will determine my future," she stated firmly.

Her father lit up and gave her arms an affectionate squeeze.

"Thank you, my love. You will enjoy yourself, you'll see," he said, practically dancing as he made his exit.

"When is this party?" Mena called after him, having forgotten to ask for one of the key details.

Sir Harvey-Morton stuck his head back into the room, still wearing that ridiculous grin.

"End of the week, so get your affairs in order," he said, and disappeared again.

"Good grief," Mena huffed, blowing an errant strand of hair off her forehead.

She turned to the window overlooking the street. An earlier rain had left the road wet, and the large puddles were illuminated by the gas lamps that lined the street. A carriage rattled by, shaking the glass in its casing. Mena rested her forehead against the window, feeling the coolness of the flat pane, comforted by its smooth firmness.

This was going to be exhausting, she knew. But she was committed now. What the hell was she going to wear? The best person to ask was her friend Thalia, but she was busy with her new husband of only a few weeks, and Mena was loath to interrupt her nuptial bliss. It seemed that Mena was on her own; something she was intimately familiar with.

Something rustled her skirts, and Mena glanced down to see her cat, Calico, rubbing himself against her leg. Mena smiled fondly and reached down to scoop him up. She snuggled into Calico's warm fur and forced herself to relax. Her first concern should be enlisting a trusted neighbor to look in on the animals. Who cared what she wore? It's not as though she was hoping to gain the duke's attention. She would bring her dreariest gowns and do her best to blend into the wallpaper.

That shouldn't be too difficult, she thought sardonically. Having been called plain her whole life, blending in came naturally.

Mena laughed softly as she carried Calico up to her bedchamber to begin packing. Imagine her, a plain mouse, trying to bewitch a powerful duke. The hilarity of the idea lifted her spirits considerably. How absurd.

✳ ✳ ✳

The carriage bounced along the road at a merry clip. Mena wished it would slow down, if only to delay the inevitable awfulness of the house party. Thankfully this one was of an abbreviated nature. In past decades house parties could last weeks at a time, but the more modern variety was just three days—four at most. She could handle that.

Mena was doubly thankful that the ride to said house party was a mere five miles away from her own home. Why, she could simply visit for the day and return to the comforts of her own bed at night. But no, her father was set on mingling with a duke and his stuffy ilk, and so Mena must suffer through it at his side. Nights included.

As the carriage rounded a corner, Mena had to grab hold of the leather handle by the window or she would have been tossed against the opposite wall. She shot her father a dark look and straightened her skirts. The carriage was a recent acquisition— a completely unnecessary one at that—and the driver was all of twelve years old. The boy's smooth cheeks had likely never felt the kiss of a razor.

Mena had wanted to pay a hack to bring them to the duke's estate, feeling magnanimous in her willingness to not insist on walking. But no, that was not good enough for her sire. The man spent money the way a grand lady might while shopping on holiday. Mena was beginning to worry that her father would end up in the workhouse over his mounting debts.

She could only hope that the situation was somehow less dire than she suspected. What did she know anyway? As a daughter she wasn't privy to much knowledge regarding finances.

Mena sniffed, stuffing down the unpleasant feelings that were beginning to surface. Giving into her frustrations and resentments solved nothing. She methodically smoothed her gray striped skirts, comforted by the motion and slippery feel of the satin fabric.

She trained her gaze out the window and focused on the lovely scenery. The sky was a brilliant blue without a single cloud to mar its perfection. The passing trees still boasted their lush greenery, but around the edges Mena spied the telltale browning that signaled the end of summer. The heat had dissipated, and the evenings were growing cool.

"I have heard the duke's sister is playing hostess this weekend," Sir Harvey-Morton said, breaking the silence Mena had been enjoying. Before long, quiet would be difficult to find in a house packed with members of the ton.

"Indeed," she replied curtly.

"Honestly, my dear, why must you be so dour? This is going to be fun."

Mena's jaw clenched for a beat, as she counted out a slow breath to maintain composure.

"I am not dour."

Her father snorted, making clear his skepticism.

"Ill-tempered, then," he replied, before loudly shifting in his seat.

"I'm not that either," Mena said, keeping her voice low enough to discourage further commentary on her emotional state.

Looking out the window, she distracted herself with thoughts of the lovely pies that would surely be served at the party. But the moment she started to relax, the trees passing by became distinctly uniform in their appearance and spacing, and the feel of the road had changed to that of a much smoother surface.

Mena felt an icy knot form in the pit of her stomach. The muscles in her thighs tightened in readiness for the moment the door swung open. This was it; she would have to become something she had long ago rejected: a refined lady. It was almost time to don her mask and take her place among the kind of people she despised.

The carriage began to slow its pace, and turned, providing a striking view of the estate house itself.

"Good Christ, what a place!" her father exclaimed, pushing himself forward to get a closer look.

Her jaw tightened as she clenched her teeth, but Mena managed to stay put and—more importantly—silent. Her father wanted to enjoy himself, and Mena would do her best to let him. She was here merely to decorate his arm, and she was already pushing it by dressing almost entirely in grays.

Sir Harvey-Morton practically jumped out of the carriage the moment the door opened. He stood, rubbing his hands together as he looked over the house as though it were a delicious pie.

Mena shook herself, trying to clear pie from her mind. But it was useless. Now she wanted to eat a pie. Perhaps there was pie inside awaiting her, along with a nice cup of expensive tea. What a cheering thought.

She scooted herself toward the door, and climbed out as gracefully as she could manage with the assistance of the young driver. The act was about to begin.

The estate house was grand and beautiful, truthfully. The main—and probably the oldest—section was a large square, three stories high, and graced with imposing marble carvings. From there a grand staircase was added to the front, and wings shot off from either side. Every inch was a cream color, which glowed in the late afternoon light. On the left, the façade was covered with some kind of vining plant, which lent an added air of romance to the whole thing.

Mena assessed the carriages that were lining the drive. Of the three that she could see, all were impeccably clean and graced with family crests. In contrast, the Harvey-Morton coach had clearly seen better days and needed some extensive painting. Not to mention the underage coachman who wore his own ill-fitting clothing, and not a uniform.

Mena braced herself for the difficulty she was about to face.

"This is going to be excellent," her father stage-whispered, and bumped her with his elbow in a jolly fashion.

"Indeed," Mena replied through her teeth, though her mind was already screaming.

Chapter

Two

Garrett peeked out his bedroom window, careful to keep himself hidden behind the curtains. It felt childish to be hiding from his own guests, and yet he couldn't bring himself to go down and face them just yet. He needed a few more minutes to prepare. And drink. He definitely needed more time to drink before he was forced to play the part of polite host.

God, what had he been thinking, hosting a house party of all things? The only reason he had agreed to this ordeal was to help his good friend, Campbell Marlowe, who had been in search of a titled bride. But everything changed when Campbell met and fell in love with Thalia Ward, a small business owner from the village. Suddenly the weekend party was no longer needed, but with plans already in motion, Garrett couldn't simply cancel the affair. Now he was stuck with a house full of young women vying for his hand. What a nightmare.

Why did men want inexperienced women in their lives, when it was easy to find a mature woman who knew what she was about in bed? Garrett thought of his mistress, who lived in London. She was unemotional about the business of pleasure, exactly the way Garrett preferred. He too was not interested in attachments and hurt feelings. He was done with bowing to the expectations of others and was determined to enjoy his life.

Though Garrett longed to bash Campbell for demanding this party be conjured into existence, he felt an absurd stab of loneliness knowing his friend was off enjoying time with his new wife. It had been nice having Campbell living at the estate, and now that he owned a home in town, Garrett missed his friend.

With a sigh, he stepped back from the window.

"Well let's get this bloody thing over with," he said, knocking back the rest of his drink.

He hissed as the amber liquid burned his throat. Good, focus on that feeling and not the feminine laughter assaulting his ears. Garrett had to force himself to step out of his rooms and close the door behind him. He took a fortifying breath and continued forward toward the fray.

He could do this. It was only a few meals, after all. He could easily avoid the majority of time spent chatting in the parlor and library, and then play a few rounds of lawn tennis. This would be simple. He was a master of avoiding bothersome women.

He was beginning to feel confident. That is, until he rounded the corner and caught a glimpse of the grand hall. There were so many women, dressed in every color of the rainbow, taking up every last inch of space. Excitement fairly crackled off the crowd. Good God, this was an enormous mistake.

Garrett's instinct was to turn tail and run before they saw him, but he knew that escape was impossible. From across the room, his sister caught his eye and waved him over. Garrett suppressed a groan and plastered a winning smile on his face. He sauntered over to greet his sister.

"Hello, Claire," Garrett said, and kissed her cheek.

Claire smiled up at him, with a devilish gleam in her eye. He knew she must be fairly bursting with pleasure at how much he was going to hate this whole enterprise. Besides, he wasn't such a terrible brother as to deny her this simple joy, even at his own expense.

"Good of you to come down, my dear brother," Claire said, and took his arm. "I shall introduce you to our guests. First, we have Lady Gwen, her mother Lady Agnes, and her sister, Lady Elizabeth."

Garrett bowed to the ladies, who dropped into deep curtsies. The two young ladies smiled at him with wide, innocent eyes, but their mother practically salivated as she looked him over. He was beginning to feel like a slab of beef at market.

Claire guided him around the hall, getting him acquainted with the assembled guests. There were thirteen families invited, and all had eagerly accepted. Disappointingly, there were only a handful of other men in attendance, and most of them were aging fathers. So, Garrett would have no camaraderie, it seemed. Unless one counted Lord Beckwith, which Garrett certainly did not.

Ever since they were classmates at school, the two men had been almost enemies. Beckwith always seemed annoyed by Garrett, no matter how charming the duke had tried to be in the past. Soon enough, Garrett had given up on establishing any kind of friendship with the other man. Now they existed in a sort of silent stalemate, neither one going out of their way to antagonize the other.

Garrett swept a critical eye over the ladies. There was a tall, stately blonde, a tall, willowy brunette, and a vivacious redhead. He would be sure to remember to speak with her. He loved redheads. In his experience they had proved to be the most fun sort.

Claire was an exceptional hostess, and somehow remembered all the names and titles of those in attendance. She glided around the room like an angel. Every sweep of her arm as graceful as a ballerina. Garrett wasn't entirely convinced that they were in fact related.

"Welcome, everyone, to Bedford House. How wonderful of you all to come. Please join us in the blue parlor for refreshments if you would like, or please feel free to retire to your rooms for a rest," Claire addressed the large group, her serene voice cutting easily through the chatter.

She turned and led the way to the parlor. Several ladies chose to see their rooms and were guided by awaiting footmen. They tittered excitedly as they ascended the stairs. Garrett hung back, waiting for the crowd to clear before following his sister. It was his duty to be present, at least in the beginning.

As he moved to exit the room, he noticed a brunette woman of medium height and build standing in the corner by the front door. She was easy to overlook, blending into the dark paneling with her dreary gown. All of the other ladies were eager to show off their best assets and flaunt their family wealth, and fussed endlessly over their hems and sleeves and hats and gloves as they crowded the foyer. Due to the chaos, the mysterious brunette had free reign to furtively watch the others with an inscrutable expression.

There was something vaguely familiar about her, but Garrett was at a complete loss to recall where they might have met previously. She looked to be the sort of woman who blended smoothly into the background wherever she went. The stiffness of her stance, along with the grim set of her mouth didn't exactly invite attention beyond a fleeting glance.

"Christ," Garrett muttered, shaking his head.

The last thing he wanted was to have some self-righteous bluestocking who didn't understand the word fun hanging around.

Perhaps she was someone's companion, or an unfortunate relation that had been dragged along. With any luck she would make herself scarce and not spoil the mood.

As he considered the stern young woman, she turned and caught him staring. She raised a brow in question, and raised her chin in defiance. Something about her made him nervous, a foreign experience for him.

Unsettled, he turned and fled to the safety of the parlor. At least he knew how to deal with the typical ladies, and he could use his sister as a shield.

* * *

Mena was shown to her room by one of the legions of footmen employed at the estate. When he theatrically opened the door for her to enter, Mena's jaw dropped. She tripped her way inside, and stared in awe at her opulent surroundings like the country bumpkin she was. The footman observed her for a moment, and then quietly excused himself, closing the door behind him with a soft click.

Mena turned in a circle, admiring the furnishings. On the bedside table sat a pretty little vase of flowers, a familiar-looking box, and a card. Mena smiled to herself as she opened the box and saw an assortment of Thalia's chocolates nestled inside. It was reassuring to have this connection to her dear friend, the local chocolatier who had provided these delicate morsels for the duke's house party. If she had to be surrounded by insufferable strangers, at least she could find comfort in the sweet treats.

She was starting to think perhaps this weekend was worth it after all, as she popped a chocolate raspberry truffle into her mouth, savoring the smooth sweet flavor.

Mena bent down and removed her boots and stockings, then stood curling her toes into the plush carpet, eyes almost closed in ecstasy. Now this was heaven. With a delighted squeal she leapt on the massive four poster bed and sank into its softness. She moaned, burying her face in the coverlet. If only she could stay here, enjoying her room, rather than rejoin the crowd downstairs.

Her stomach grumbled, reminding her that dinner would be her reward for the torture that awaited. She flopped over onto her back, swiped hair from her eyes and huffed in frustration. At least there was time for a bath. By the door was a bellpull, which would bring servants running to see to her comfort. Ridiculous, really, but she might as well enjoy it for a few days.

This first evening would be the ladies' chance to show off their charms. Mena was thoroughly relieved that she was exempt from such displays. She was here merely as a companion to her father. As someone who wanted to blend in with the surroundings, Mena selected a dove gray dinner gown and a simple strand of pearls to wear closely around her throat.

She wanted no further ornamentation, which her assigned maid strongly disapproved of. The young woman scowled at Mena's refusal to festoon herself with jewels and ribbons. No amount of cajoling would change her mind though, and soon the maid gave up and departed after putting Mena's hair up in a simple yet elegant arrangement of twists and braids.

Mena turned her face side to side, admiring the updo. It was certainly much prettier than she could have accomplished on her own, but the heap of hair pins was already giving her a headache as they pulled and poked at her scalp. Sadly, Mena wasn't vain enough to put up with this kind of lifestyle. She would rather be outside with the dogs or reading a book in a comfortable frock.

"Well, here it goes," she told her reflection with a sigh.

She left her room and retraced her previous steps back down to the great hall. The sound of people talking floated down the hall, and Mena allowed it to lead her to the drawing room, where many members of the house party were already assembled for a drink.

The pre-dinner cocktail was a fairly new custom, and excitement rippled through the crowd as they accepted and tasted the concoction. Mena was curious, but she eyed her chilled glass of strange pink liquid with suspicion before sipping at it. It was surprisingly good, though she could already feel the alcohol warming her blood. Mena almost never drank. It loosened her tight grip on herself, and she despised that loss of control.

Her father had no such scruples, and eagerly downed his second glass under Mena's watchful gaze across the room. She sincerely hoped to avoid an embarrassing situation, but it was out of her hands now. The tension in her shoulders increased, and she was hit with a nearly knee-buckling wave of exhaustion. Her corset certainly didn't help matters.

"Ah, Sir Harvey-Morton! Thank you for coming to our party," a deep, masculine voice called out from somewhere across the crowded room. Mena's father turned and located the speaker. He flushed in pleasure and bowed deeply.

"The pleasure is mine, of course, your grace," he said.

Mena's stomach flipped. It was the duke himself. She did not want to be waved over and then stuck beside her father while he sidled up to the duke. Sensing an opportunity to avoid being seen, she drifted farther away unnoticed. She made it to the heavy velvet curtains by the window and tucked herself in beside them, trying to blend in.

"Miss Harvey-Morton! Welcome," an arrestingly beautiful young woman said as she approached, appearing to glide across the floor rather than walk like a mere mortal. "I am his grace's sister, Lady Claire. It is lovely to make your acquaintance."

Mena dipped a curtsy, her body invariably following the rules of proper deportment without involving her mind at all. The woman before her was young, probably in her early twenties, with luscious golden curls piled high in an artful coiffure and adorned with pearls and clear crystals. Her heart shaped face, rosebud lips, and wide blue eyes were as flawless as a porcelain doll.

"Thank you for the invitation, my lady," Mena replied, shifting uncomfortably, her voice quiet but steady.

Often at gatherings she suffered a crippling sensation, not unlike suffocation, but she was holding herself together this time—for now. She looked at the woman before her. If she wasn't mistaken, her smile seemed to be truly genuine. Mena surprised herself by smiling a little in return. Apparently, her lessons from finishing school took over whether she liked it or not.

"I shall introduce you around." The woman took Mena's arm without waiting for a response and led her back to the group. "Here is Lady Grandall with her daughter, Lady Jane. Here is Lady Marsdown with her daughter, Lady Constance…"

Mena lost track of the names and titles at that point and began thinking about what dinner might consist of. She was looking forward to the endless courses that such dinners entailed. Most people dreaded having to sit for so long, the boring stilted conversation, and such. But Mena could easily avoid conversation and simply enjoy eating. No one wanted to speak with her for long, once they realized how subdued she was.

The only inescapable flaw in the structure of a lavish dinner was that one must stop eating when the host stopped. Thus, if your host was finicky or tyrannical, everyone else was forced to leave most of their food untouched. Mena couldn't stand food waste, especially when it was lovely food. But her hostess seemed to be a kind soul. Surely, she wouldn't deny her guests their fill. Mena would just have to hope.

Three

Garrett sat at the head of the long dining table and observed his guests over the rim of his wine glass. He was feeling loose from the drinks he had consumed but had plenty of experience with the stuff to handle himself. Almost every guest was sneaking glances at him when they thought he wasn't looking. It was all so exhausting. He really only liked company when he wasn't hosting and could leave at will. This was...too much.

What course was it? He had lost track. Garrett squinted down at his plate, trying to ascertain what he had just eaten. Some kind of vegetable? He couldn't be sure. The dim lighting didn't help.

'Your grace," came a voice at his elbow.

Garrett turned, remembering to flash a smooth smile at his guest.

"Yes, Lady Jane?"

The matron by his elbow blushed prettily and shot a look at her daughter who sat nearby. Clearly the mother wanted her daughter to use this seating advantage to ingratiate herself with the duke. Garrett looked down the table to his sister, fighting the panic. Claire raised a brow and suppressed a smirk before turning back to converse with her table neighbors. Always elegant, she waded through high society with an easy grace.

"Are the men going to be deserting us ladies at the end of the meal, or shall we be expecting your company, your grace?" the matron asked with a flirtatious smile, and eyelids that couldn't stop flapping at him.

Garrett swallowed a groan. Claire had warned him earlier that he wouldn't be able to escape so easily and would be required to entertain his guests in the parlor after dinner. For one night only. Then he would be able to make the usual excuses and retreat to the billiard room with the other men. He forced a charming smile to his reticent lips.

"I don't intend to neglect you so callously, Lady Jane. After dinner we shall all retire to the parlor together. Perhaps you would be so bold as to join me for a game of bridge?"

The matron blushed quite fetchingly, and practically bounced in her seat.

"Oh yes, your grace. I would be most honored. My daughter is an excellent bridge player as well."

She nodded to her daughter, who flashed Garrett a look that reminded him of a startled deer. He felt sympathy for the poor girl, who clearly wasn't any match for her mother's machinations.

"I confess to being a novice card player, but I would be honored by the chance to be soundly beaten by you, Miss Humboldt," Garrett said, turning up the charm to soothe the frightened chit.

The girl's eyes widened even further, and she chewed her lower lip. Her eyes darted over to her mother before returning to him, and she jerked her head in a nod.

"Thank you, your grace," she squeaked out, and then directed her gaze down to her plate.

Garrett exhaled slowly through his nose, working hard to keep his expression impassive, though he longed to escape. Taking a large sip of wine, he looked down the long table at the assembled guests. They appeared engrossed in their conversations, and largely ignored their plates. Most especially the women of the group, who seemed to be in competition to eat the least amount of food.

All except one woman, who spoke to no one and ate heartily. She seemed in good cheer as she tucked into her meal. Garrett felt a kinship with the woman, as he was a food lover himself. If not for all these spectators watching his every move, he would be shoveling the food in and asking for seconds. God, he missed his solitude.

Suddenly the woman looked over at him, and when she caught him staring, a rosy blush stained her cheeks. Garrett hastily looked away, feeling sorry for having embarrassed her. One shouldn't stare at their guests, and all that. He recognized her from when she had arrived earlier. She had exchanged her gray striped dress for one equally drab and wore no adornment.

When he couldn't control his curiosity anymore, he glanced over and saw that she had set her cutlery aside and was sitting silently, hands in her lap. Damn, he'd ruined her meal. Feeling guilty, Garrett decided to try and covertly send a tray up to her room later. But first he would have to figure out which one she was. Surely Claire would know; she knew everything.

Eventually the table was cleared, and the tablecloth removed to reveal a more intricate lace one beneath. Platters piled high with various fruit and nuts were brought in by the footmen, and the butler set about providing new glasses for port and sherry.

The guests all murmured in appreciation as the desserts were placed on the table'—towering puddings and jellies studded with tropical fruits from the estate hothouse.

Garrett was counting down the minutes until this ordeal was over. He tried to send his sister a meaningful look, in the hopes she would stand up and announce the ladies' departure, but she was studiously avoiding eye contact and was instead holding court at her end of the table, sure to leave several broken male hearts in her wake.

After an interminable length of time, Lady Claire finally rose, signaling to all that the ladies would be retiring to the parlor. The gentlemen all jumped up to assist the ladies with their chairs, and once the last set of silk skirts swished out the door, the men began to follow them out. Garrett was less enthusiastic about continuing to entertain, but he couldn't escape just yet.

* * *

Mena followed the other ladies to the parlor, where they each selected a seat with the intention of displaying themselves for the duke's perusal. Each was eager to attract his attention, and hopefully his hand in marriage. Since she was decidedly not trying to attract the duke's attention, Mena chose to sit by the windows that overlooked the gardens, though it was too dark now to see them.

The curtains provided some sense of separation, and she longed for a book to read while the other ladies chattered about fashion and the most recent gossip. Instead, she was left people watching, which was a pleasant enough pastime, but she didn't want to attract interest by being caught staring either. It was a delicate balance; one she had plenty of experience with.

"Who do you think the duke will set his sights on?" one of the ladies asked the others sitting close to her.

She used her fan as a shield to gossip behind, green eyes flashing with excitement as she spoke. This was the absolute zenith of upper crust feminine pastimes, considering their options were tragically minimal. Instead of pursuing some sort of uplifting hobby, ladies were reduced to tearing each other down over the most minor of social transgressions. Like daring to desire the hand of a duke, for example. Though, of course, that was what they were all present for, whether they would admit it or not.

"You know as well as I that the duke has no interest in marrying. It's curious he bothered to invite us all here," another one replied, keeping her voice low.

This intrigued Mena, who knew nothing of London society. Why did the duke not wish to marry? He was a handsome man, perhaps he enjoyed his freedom too much. She would certainly never want to be in the position of vying for the hand of a man who had no interest in entangling his future with her own.

"Rumor has it, the dowager duchess is on her way to England from her travels abroad," the first lady was saying to her compatriots.

"Suppose she is forcing his hand?" the second lady asked, eyes alight with interest in the private lives of other people.

"I'm sure her grace expected grandchildren long ago," the first lady replied with a self-satisfied smile.

Murmurs of agreement from the group ended the conversation, just as the men made their way back from the dining room. Mena looked at the duke with fresh eyes, wondering at his internal workings. She shouldn't find him as interesting as she did and attempted to chalk it up entirely to his good looks.

There was a stiffness in how he held himself, as though bracing for the onslaught of feminine attention he surely received everywhere he went. It was impossible for a man like him not to be swooned over constantly. It probably went to the man's head, making him arrogant and insufferable. Though Mena could see a hunted look in his blue eyes that struck a chord in her soul. She understood how it felt to be an oddity among a crowd, though for very different reasons than a powerful duke.

The duke hesitated near one of the large potted ferns positioned on either side of the door, the green stems rising up from enormous Chinese urns which were likely real antiques. The aristocracy had gone through an obsession with the far East in past decades, seemingly stripping the countries across the sea of every last item of artistic value. Mena wondered what had been left behind, and how the locals would feel if they could see where their historical items had ended up.

She knew she shouldn't spare a moment of concern over the shadows apparent beneath the duke's strikingly blue eyes, but she couldn't fully squash the spurt of empathy from her soft heart as she looked him over, taking in the evidence of the man's exhaustion. The other ladies were right, it made no sense that the duke had invited them all here. And Mena knew his secret—he did not truly mean to take a wife.

The duke had intended this event to be an opportunity for his friend Campbell Marlowe to find a titled bride. But their plans had gone awry when Marlowe instead fell in love with Thalia Ward, Mena's close friend. It was this knowledge that had compelled Mena to give in to her father's desire to come here, safe in the knowledge that the duke wasn't on the marriage market. And neither was she.

***

Garrett lurked in the hallway behind a large potted fern after the other men had all gone into the parlor. He knew that duty required him to make an appearance and entertain his guests, but he was exhausted from all the socializing he'd already been through. And his face hurt from smiling. Blast, this was harder than he'd expected. This was why he never entertained.

In London, he gladly accepted invitations to dinners, balls, soirees, the opera...but when one was merely a guest, they had the freedom to leave on a whim. And a duke could largely do as he liked without anyone judging him. Having no distinct political ambitions helped too.

This weekend was quite the ordeal. He would rather have walked over hot coals and spent the weekend in the hospital. Was that an option? Perhaps he should get himself arrested. Surely then he would have a worthy excuse to avoid spending any more time entertaining these jackals.

But no, he sighed. That would just cause more problems, and Claire would never forgive him.

Garrett braced himself for the onslaught of feminine attention and walked into the parlor with full ducal swagger. Instantly every head turned to look at him, and Garrett pasted on a dashing smile for his unwelcome audience.

"Anyone for a game of whist?" he asked, rubbing his hands together.

Every female face lit up, all of them wanting him to partner with them. Garrett wanted to kick himself. He looked around, trying to find a path through this delicate situation. Claire wouldn't do, nor would any of the gentlemen. Then his gaze landed on the woman in gray with the hearty appetite. She was sitting on the window seat trying to blend in with the curtains. She would do perfectly. Garrett crossed the room, feeling the eyes boring into his back as he did so, and stopped before the woman. She looked up at him with a blank expression.

"I would be honored to have you as my partner, my lady."

He executed an elegant bow, hoping to make her blush. But when she didn't respond, Garrett just stood there, starting to feel awkward. Surely, she wouldn't refuse him, unless she couldn't play.

"If you do not know the rules, I would be happy to teach you. It is quite simple," he added with a winning smile.

The woman continued to stare at him for a moment before looking past him at the observers. Then she had the audacity to look resigned as she stood.

"Not a lady, just a miss," she said in a quiet voice Garrett almost couldn't hear.

"Ah—"

"Thank you, your grace, for the invitation," she said, squaring her shoulders as though about to face a battle.

Garrett, feeling thoroughly confused, led her to one of the card tables set up for playing, and held out her chair. She sat, hands in her lap, and looked like she would rather be anywhere else but here. It was starting to rankle, to be honest. Garrett was not usually subject to this kind of rejection.

"And who will join us?" he asked, standing by his chair, ready to sit.

There was an audible sigh from the other ladies in the room as Lord Beckwith smoothly rushed to claim one of the remaining seats, along with a young lady who could only have been the man's sister. They could have been twins, except for the fine lines already appearing on the gentleman's face. They were both elegant and classically beautiful, with blond curls and pale green eyes.

Garrett wondered why he couldn't recall having met the lady before, having known Beckwith for years. Honestly, he struggled to keep track of the many titles he was supposed to have memorized. Not that had he ever put much effort into bothering to learn anyone's name. Behind Garrett's table, Lady Claire was organizing the others into tables the footmen were busy helping arrange. Garrett picked up the neat stack of cards in the center of their table and began to shuffle them.

"My, you are so good at handling the cards, your grace," the lady to Garrett's left proclaimed with saccharine breathlessness.

She smiled inanely and was already grating on Garrett's nerves. Looking across the table to Beckwith, Garrettcaught a flicker of annoyance in the man's expression.

Garrett slid his gaze to the lady across the table, whose face was unreadable. Deliberately so. But the moment her eyes met his, there appeared a crack in her fortress, as the corner of her mouth turned up. A distinct glimmer of suppressed amusement appeared in her eyes, and Garrett wanted to bask in the moment, thoroughly pleased to be deemed worthy of this simple connection.

Thankfully Beckwith jumped to speak, saving Garrett the awkwardness of thinking of a response to whatever it was his sis sister had said.

"Quite so. We are so grateful to be selected to test your skills, your grace. Lady Desmonia and I are well practiced at whist, are we not, Sister?"

The hard edge to his words made clear the man's disdain, lest Garrett forget for a moment the reason why Beckwith disliked him. Which was honestly difficult, as Garrett didn't really know from what Beckwith's annoyance with him originated, other than a general sense of jealousy. Lord knew Garrett would have been happy to trade places with the other man, to spare himself the abuse his father had inflicted over the years as the late duke attempted to shape his heir into a proper gentleman.

Lady Desmonia smiled demurely, but her slight smile revealed an arrogance that was off-putting. No man with any pride would want a woman simpering at him with faux reverence.

Garrett hastened to deal out the cards, thirteen each, and laid the last card down face up to begin the round. A game or two, hurriedly played, and he could be free from this ordeal and back in his rooms in peace.

Lady Desmonia put a card in the center of the table.

"I'm afraid we are not yet acquainted," she said, looking at Garrett's partner as she spoke. "I am Lady Desmonia and this is my brother, Lord Beckwith."

"I am Miss Harvey-Morton, the vicar's daughter," the other lady said flatly, and met Garrett's gaze with her own direct stare. Her expression remained perfectly bland as she leaned forward to lay down her own card.

"Pleased to make your acquaintance, Miss Harvey-Morton," Lord Beckwith replied with a grating smile as he tossed his card on the stack.

Garrett tucked the trump card into his hand and put a card down.

"I hope you are well settled and are finding your accommodations to your liking."

She looked up from her cards at him, a startled expression crossing her face before her stoic expression was back in place. A delicate pink blush crept onto her high cheekbones as her eyes dropped quickly back down.

"My rooms are quite comfortable and lovely. Thank you, your grace," she replied softly, her chin tucked into her chest as though hiding.

Lord Beckwith slid the cards over to him, having won the first trick, and put down a new card. Garrett threw down another and sat back in his chair. A footman was slowly circulating around with a tray of refreshments, but too far away from their table. Blast.

"And what excitement do you have planned for us on the morrow, your grace?" Lady Desmonia asked with a decidedly flirtatious tone.

Garrett suppressed a groan and forced a smile to his lips in an attempt to maintain the facade of a cheerful host, and said,

"The men are going to go shooting in the morning, and then my sister has planned a picnic for everyone."

"Oh, how lovely," Lady Desmonia practically squealed. "Let the men have their fun while we ladies have a lie in. But tell me there will be dancing after dinner."

Garrett raised his brows. Lord, he hoped there wouldn't be dancing, but he couldn't remember whether or not he had made this clear to Claire when they had discussed plans for the weekend.

This could get even worse tomorrow.

He wouldn't survive.

"I shall ask Lady Claire what she has planned for us, my lady. The lady of the house is the real head of the household, as we all know," he said smoothly.

Across the table Miss Harvey-Morton was watching him. She reminded Garrett of a cat, all silent grace and unforgiving haughtiness. She held herself apart—aloof—and it was difficult to view that as anything other than feeling superior. Perhaps she was a bluestocking who thought herself more intelligent than other people.

How boring. Garrett loathed being lectured by bookish women. He preferred the more entertaining variety, though he wanted genuine intellect, not cloying vapidness like the debutantes he was suffering through now. They were like spun sugar—no substance and far too sweet.

The round completed and Lady Desmonia won the trick. She smiled with self-satisfaction and placed her next card down with a firm slap. Miss Harvey-Morton put down hers, and around it went, before Garrett won. Maybe his partner didn't know how to play the game? Garrett was beginning to worry for her.

But the fourth round revealed that Miss Harvey-Morton did know how to play, and she was quite good. Her stoic expression never faltered, as she handily won the next four rounds. Lady

Desmonia and her brother were looking less confident with each win for Miss Harvey-Morton. Garrett found himself entertaining the idea of teaching this vicar's daughter to play poker.

"Well done, Miss-Harvey-Morton. You are a regular card sharp," Garrett said with a laugh as he watched her rake in yet another win.

Garrett noticed the barest hint of a smile lifting the left corner of her rosebud mouth, and he felt triumph race through him.

"Thank you, your grace. I played often in school."

"That explains it. Well, I will endeavor to not feel entirely sorry for myself later. I was busy with other pursuits in school."

He shot her a challenging look over his hand of cards and was rewarded when her blush deepened. She tore her gaze away from his and looked down at her cards. Garrett could see her throat working, like she wanted to speak. But she didn't.

Instead, Beckwith broke in and said, "You might remember, Sumner, that I was there during those schoolboy adventures."

Garrett gritted his teeth. He would prefer not to think about the years the men had been forced into such close proximity, and how they once might have been friends.

"Perhaps you might enlighten us about the sort of activity you engaged in," Miss Harvey-Morton suggested, as calmly as a person might comment on the weather.

What was he supposed to say to that, he wondered. Garrett shot Beckwith a hard look before letting out a chuckle and donning a charming smile.

"Nothing I would dare admit aloud."

Lady Desmonia giggled, far too delighted by his statement. It was not a flirtation aimed at her, though she seemed ready to misinterpret even the slightest deference.

The reality of the situation slammed into him then, as Garrett saw how much these ladies wanted to become his duchess. One false move could end up shackling him forever to one of these huntresses.

Thankfully, the game was coming to an end. Relief coursed through him as Beckwith and his sister set down the rest of their cards. But then Miss Harvey-Morton stood, and immediately excused herself. Without a backward glance, she strode away from the table, perhaps headed to her room. Garrett stared after her for a moment, oddly disappointed to lose her company.

"I would love to play again, your grace," Lady Desmonia said, pulling his attention away from the empty doorway as she and her brother stood.

"Of course," Garrett managed to say, distractedly.

She sank into a curtsy, before moving back to the safety of the herd of similar young ladies filling up the sitting room. Swallowing hard, Garrett nodded stiffly to Beckwith, then went to find Claire. It was safer to stand imposingly behind her chair while she entertained with typical effortless grace. She was a wall of protection between Garrett and their guests.

Once the clock finally chimed for the hour, Garrett swiftly kissed Claire on the cheek and slipped away, practically running for the stairs. He had spent plenty of time with everyone tonight. Surely no one would be too put out by his absence.

As soon as he was safely behind the door of his ducal chambers, Garrett removed his neckcloth and jacket. He sat in one of the leather chairs in his private sitting room and rolled up his sleeves.

A decanter of whiskey and a crystal glass sat waiting for him, along with a box of Thalia's chocolates. Garrett picked up the small blue box and shook it, listening to the rustling that came from within. At least he had something to eat with his whiskey, he thought as he tossed the box back on the table and poured himself a drink.

Knowing that tomorrow would be a longer, more trying day did nothing to help his mood. Garrett groaned as he lay his head back against the top of his chair, squeezing his eyes shut. He didn't appreciate having to hide in his rooms either. Usually, Garrett spent his lonely nights in the library reading—drinking mostly, if he were being honest—and he wasn't accustomed to going to bed this early.

He gulped down his drink and refilled his glass. Maybe if he waited for a while everyone would begin to head to bed. Surely those who had traveled a distance to be here would enjoy an early night, he reasoned. He would just have a few drinks and then he would try and head down for a book, when the risk of bumping into someone was low.

Chapter

Four

Close to midnight, Mena tossed and turned in her bed. The mattress was either too firm or too soft, she couldn't decide. The pillows were overly large and made her neck sore. She was too cold with one blanket, but two made her hot. She fussed around in the bed, spinning about until her nightgown was all tangled around her legs.

Sighing in frustration, Mena struggled to free herself and sit up. She looked out at the bright round moon glowing outside her window. The moon had often felt like her one companion and confidant when she had been stuck at finishing school, especially after Ashley had left. Mena had often lain awake in bed, whispering all her secrets to the moon when she had no one to share them with.

What did she need to tell the moon tonight? That this house did not feel like a home. It was enormous and had an achingly empty feeling. It was lonely here, and she felt too exposed and scrutinized. Crowds often made her feel uneasy and needing to flee in a panic. She missed the comfort of Calico and her aging dog, Gruff, both of whom often shared her bed.

Mena was an outsider here—an interloper—come to survey foreign territory. Of course, the other ladies didn't know that, and likely assumed she was just another eager contender for the duke's attention. It was helpful that Mena was no great beauty, and thus was easily ignored, but she worried about the wrath of the others. No one was as brutal as a lady on the hunt for a handsome gentleman.

But Mena didn't even want to be here. She wasn't trying to marry the duke, and she had no interest in climbing into the heights of the aristocracy anyway. She blew out a frustrated huff of air, lifting the lock of brown hair that had fallen across her forehead.

Perhaps reading would help ease her into sleep. It had often worked while she was at school. Mena searched her bedside table but found nothing. She couldn't remember if she had brought a book with her, but searching her trunk, she also found nothing. Blast, she would be forced to go down to peruse the library if she wanted to read.

She would have to go alone. At night. In this giant, probably haunted, mansion. Her teeth chattered at the thought, but she forced herself out of bed and into slippers and a thick cotton wrap that covered her from chin to toe. If only she had Gruff with her, she wouldn't be so ready to jump at every shadow.

Mena opened her door and stuck her head out, looking to see if anyone was walking about out there. Thankfully the hall was empty, and the wall was illuminated with a neat row of gaslights turned down to a cozy glow. She left her door ajar and crept down the hall as quietly as possible, keeping close to the wall.

Down the stairs to the main floor, she struggled to remember which direction it was. Shadows stretched across the floor, seeming to leap out toward her. Mena schooled herself not to jump at every shadow. It wasn't her fault that this huge empty house was frightening. It looked like the setting of a tragic gothic novel. But something far more terrifying lurked here—members of the ton.

She made a guess and turned left, following the hall, passing several rooms before finally reaching the library. She could see books through the open door though the lights were turned down very low. Pleased that she had found her way, Mena stepped cautiously into the room, ready to run away at the sight of any ghosts. Encountering nothing strange, she turned the gaslights up, illuminating the rows of bookshelves that lined the four walls and went up to dizzying heights.

Mena relaxed her shoulders and stood up straighter. Nothing here but glorious books. Now to find a suitable one to help her relax, and she could be on her way back to the safety of her bed. She scanned the shelves, using her finger to smooth over the titles as she went. There were plenty of farming books on the shelves, more than one would expect a duke to have in his private collection. They were given a place of prominence, displacing the standard classics most aristocrats collected for display.

She continued along until finally she saw some familiar titles. Shakespeare, the Greek and Roman classics, and a large collection of poetry. What would make her fall asleep the quickest? Surely a weighty book of romantic drivel would do the job, she reasoned as she slid a copy of Robert Browning's poetry out and hefted it in her arms. Perhaps she should take something else as well, just in case this first one didn't do the trick.

Mena slid out a slimmer title from the shelf just above her head. It was bound in red leather with a difficult to decipher script on the cover. Mena turned with the books in her arms toward the door. Feeling quite accomplished for her success, she was about to leave when she cried out in surprise, laying eyes on the duke asleep in one of the heavy leather chairs. He jolted awake in an instant at the sound of her screech and was on his feet looking alert but confused.

"What's going on?" he demanded, his gaze sweeping over the room, searching for danger.

Mena noticed that his speech was a touch slurred, whether from sleep or drink, she wasn't sure. She swallowed, trying to control her racing heart.

"Your grace, I didn't see you there. I came to take a book and you surprised me. My apologies."

She clutched the larger book to her chest, but she had dropped the smaller volume. The duke's shirt was undone, sleeves rolled up over his elbows, exposing the paler skin beneath. Mena struggled to keep her eyes locked on his face rather than his nearly nude torso. Unfortunately, she couldn't help a brief flick of her eyes over his lean muscled body, and she felt her cheeks heat, hoping that he was unaware of her reaction. Surely, he was accustomed to ladies falling all over themselves to get his attention, she thought bitterly.

The duke stared at her, blinking for a moment and she couldn't guess his thoughts. Finally, he passed a hand over his head, ruffling his golden hair.

"It is I who should apologize, Miss Harvey-Morton," he said, and bent down to retrieve the book she had dropped.

He studied the cover, turning it over. The hair hanging rakishly across his brow nearly obscured his left eye as he looked up at her. It gave him a rather piratical appearance, especially with his tight trousers stretching over powerfully muscled thighs. He exuded masculine power and confidence. Damn him.

Mena struggled to control her physical reaction to him. It wasn't personal, it was only a natural biological response to an arousing situation, she told herself, aiming for a scientific view of things. Animal attraction, that was all it was. But her body wasn't aware that it was supposed to remain impersonal, and she found herself overheating and in need of…something. Some kind of relief.

"That particular book might not be to your liking," he warned, a peculiar gleam in his eye as he held it out for her to take.

Mena reached out for it and was unnerved when the duke did not let go right away. He held her gaze for a beat, then released his grip on the book, casually sliding his hands into his pockets.

"Why wouldn't I like it?" Mena asked, her voice sounding oddly breathless to her own ears.

She scowled, hoping to scare him off, the way an animal might. She tried to imagine herself as an unlovable badger, rather than a cat in heat, which was more akin to the sensation she was actually experiencing. Despite what her rational mind was trying to tell her, she longed to curl around his body, pressing and rubbing herself on him. But truthfully, Mena would rather be a grumpy weasel who lived alone in the safety of her private burrow, thank you very much.

The duke smiled slyly and rocked back on his heels.

"It is the memoir of a famous rake, Viscount Humboldt. It would shock you immensely with its vulgarity."

The words were tossed like a gauntlet, daring Mena to prove that she wasn't some withering debutante.

"That is the very reason that I selected it, your grace," she replied calmly, hoping her superior expression was convincing.

He broke out in a blinding grin that threatened to buckle Mena's knees. How could one man be this gorgeous? It wasn't fair. Mena had to remain impervious to it, and to his flirtatious nature. She lifted her chin.

"Is there anything else I can assist you with, Miss Harvey-Morton?"

"Mena," she surprised herself by saying.

The duke stilled. His green eyes traveled over her as though seeing her for the first time. Then he smiled, looking pleased.

"Garrett."

"Garrett," she repeated softly, shyly.

"Mena."

His deep voice saying her name was so sensual, Mena wanted to throw herself against him and feel his mouth against hers, hear him say her name again with passion. She shook her head slightly, clearing her head of such lustful thoughts. What was happening to her?

It was perfectly logical, really, and should be easily controlled. He was an attractive man, and Mena was merely reacting to it as one did. There, now she should be able to keep a cool head.

"I—I should go to bed. Goodnight," Mena spluttered, feeling decidedly the opposite of logical.

She managed to walk on wobbly knees across the library to the door. She avoided looking directly at the duke as she went and was nearly out the door when he spoke again.

"Good evening, Mena."

She nodded jerkily in response.

Good lord, she was in trouble, Mena thought as she fled.

Five

The next morning Garrett rose late, suffering a slight headache from his excessive drinking the night before. He sent his valet to bring him a breakfast tray to avoid going down to dine with the guests. His head couldn't handle all that just yet. But along with his valet came Claire, encased in a high collared lavender gown with several ridiculous lacy flounces.

"Good morning," she sang as she walked in, heading straight to the windows still covered with their heavy curtains.

Claire threw back the curtains, allowing in the brilliant late summer sun, and burning Garrett's eyes in the process. He winced and covered his eyes with a groan.

"Hey, that's a bit much," he protested.

Claire continued until all four windows in the room were uncovered. Then she sat primly on the settee and poured Garrett a cup of tea from the breakfast tray, handing him a cup with practiced grace.

"Thank you," he said gently, and sipped the hot liquid.

It did help his head ache less, which was something. Claire tapped her fingers on the arm of the settee.

"You begged me to help you with this party," she reminded him. "I didn't come up with this idea by myself."

Claire leaned back, addressing her complaint to the ceiling. Garrett felt a sliver of guilt crawl through him, but he shrugged it off. How many times has he helped Claire in the past? Sure, this party wasn't what it had been intended to be, but it was hardly Garrett's fault that Campbell had demanded this party to find himself a wealthy bride and then skipped out on it with a village woman on his arm, leaving Garrett to keep up the charade of looking for a wife.

Damn the man for finding love and leaving Garrett behind to deal with this mess. And the feelings rising up were not jealousy. Absolutely not. Garrett despised the institution of marriage. His own parents, and practically everyone around him, confirmed the dubious nature of the system. But he wished Campbell all the best with his new bride.

"I know, I know," Garrett replied, rubbing his sore eyes.

"I do have a life, Garrett. I cannot simply drop everything to come here at your every whim. Nor can I spend weeks planning a party for absolutely no reason at all. What a waste of my time and talents," Claire grumbled, warming to her subject.

Garrett felt himself getting defensive, and steeled himself for the lengthy lecture that was coming. At times it seemed as if his younger sister lived to berate him.

"I was trying to help Campbell. He forced me! None of this was my doing," Garrett protested, knowing it made no difference to Claire, who was forced to play out this sham of a party regardless.

"And the man has conveniently disappeared from the estate just in time, it seems," she said sardonically.

Her elegantly arched brows were drawn together, but even glowering she still looked like a golden angel. Garrett couldn't help teasing her.

"And what would you be doing, if not this? Something of immense importance, like shopping or attending the opera? Dancing with some knob you hope to ensnare?"

He grinned at her scowl and then had to duck the pillow she threw at him in a huff. The pillow bounced off his chair and smashed a priceless Chinese vase on the floor. Garrett turned back to Claire with raised brows. She crossed her arms defiantly.

"I blame you for that as well," she sniffed, chin lifted.

"You would," he replied, but he didn't care enough about the decor to comment further. There were countless more priceless vases where that one had come from.

They sat in silence for a few moments.

"Are truly none of them to your liking?" Claire finally asked. "I thought one or two might strike your fancy."

Garrett wrinkled his brow in confusion.

"Who? What are you talking about?"

Claire rolled her eyes.

"The ladies. I invited them for *you* to consider, not just Campbell."

"Umm, why? You know I have no interest in marriage," Garrett replied. "I've done my best not to notice them so far."

He was surprised that Claire was playing matchmaker for him. She of all people should understand his aversion to marriage, having grown up in the same house.

"You must marry eventually, Garrett," she said softly.

"Why is that?" he laughed.

Claire looked up at him, incredulous.

"You are the duke. There must be an heir. It isn't really about you, or what you want."

Garrett felt the familiar sinking feeling in his chest at her words, and the pressure that came along with such privilege. She didn't know how it felt, nor could she. It wasn't her fault they had been born into their perspective stations, and Claire had her own cross to bear. Garrett fought down his rising panic until he could speak again with his usual nonchalance.

"There must be some distant relative to inherit. Or the crown will simply retake possession of the lands. It is not my problem," he said dismissively.

Claire frowned at him.

"And what of the tenants? The village? You would leave them all to the whims of someone else? Someone who cares nothing for them?" she demanded, voice dripping with scorn.

Garrett shrugged and took a bite of the cheese scone on his breakfast tray.

"I don't owe anyone anything, most especially my very life and future," he said around a mouthful of food.

"Duty."

The word landed like a brick through a window. Garrett's fingers curled into a fist on his lap until he felt the bite of his fingernails in his palm. He released a slow, controlled breath.

"Let's not have this conversation, Claire. Please," he said.

She studied him for a moment.

"Tonight, we will have dancing after dinner. I am allowing you and the other gentlemen to go shooting today, so get your fresh air in before you are confined to the house," she said, changing the subject.

"How generous of you," Garrett said dryly.

"I am, thank you," she smiled, her blue eyes dancing with mischief. "And you will participate in the dancing, of course."

Garrett groaned.

"Alright, but I'm not dancing with all of them. There's far too many."

"If you don't, some will take it as special attention," she warned.

"I don't care."

Claire shrugged.

"Five ladies then," she said.

"Two."

"Four."

"Three."

Claire smiled in triumph and clapped her hands together.

"Three it is then! And I honestly didn't think I could even get you to dance with that many."

"Should I reconsider and not dance at all? I don't even like shooting," he grumbled.

"It's not about the shooting, as you well know. It's a chance to escape the ladies. Three dances with three different partners. And none of them me," she said.

Garrett grinned. His sister was too intelligent to trick.

"I agree to your terms, though I preferred it when you were younger and I could out maneuver you."

Claire beamed and reached out to shake on it. Her delicate hands were marred by a single callus on the side of her middle finger. Garrett raised a brow in question as he touched the rough skin. Claire shook her head slightly and pulled away. Apparently, this wasn't a topic of conversation either for now. She was an enigma.

"Well, I need to be off, preparing for the picnic later. Enjoy shooting things with the other men," she rolled her eyes as she stood and smoothed her skirts.

Garrett waved her off, and then sat for a moment staring into the empty fireplace. The day was warm, with a freshness to the air. He wasn't a particular fan of hunting or shooting, but it was an excuse to get outside, and most especially, avoid the ladies. He couldn't spend a whole day being hounded by marriage minded women. Thank God none of the other men talked overly much. Even Lord Beckwith proved less of a chatterbox when his sister wasn't around.

* * *

Mena woke early, despite having slept poorly. After returning to her room, she had been too stirred up to fall asleep right away, and her poor choice of books hadn't leant itself to that end either. Feeling jittery and uncomfortable, Mena had gone outside to breathe the fresh air and settle her nerves. The fields around the estate were smothered by fog in the early morning light. The distant sound of sheep bleating brought a smile to her face, and she set out to find them.

The other ladies were assembled in the parlor when Mena returned from her walk. She hadn't bothered to change, knowing that she would be required to change once again before long. Perhaps she would take a nap and have a bath after a light repast and several cups of delicious, expensive ducal tea. Her stomach growled as she found a seat in an unoccupied chair, and she was excited to taste some cakes and biscuits. There was a gorgeous three-tiered display of tiny frosted cakes, thick sliced shortbread biscuits, and apple tarts.

Mena eagerly filled a small plate with a selection of treats, ready to enjoy them. She caught several side-eyed judgmental glances from some of the other ladies. She noticed that no one else was eating anything, they were instead sedately sipping their tea. Perhaps the food wasn't very good? Mena took an experimental nibble of a cake and had to stifle an unladylike moan of pleasure at the burst of flavor. Whoever made these cakes should be given an award. She practically gobbled the rest of it down and had to remind herself sternly to eat slowly and not shovel more in after it.

"Was that cake very good?" a quiet voice by her left elbow ventured. Mena turned in surprise.

"Yes, it was amazing! I've never had one so good," she replied enthusiastically. "You must try one."

The young woman who had spoken looked longingly at the cake, but didn't reach for one. Mena noticed her pronounced collarbones, and angular cheeks beneath sad eyes. Her expression pulled at Mena's heart, and she was instantly transported back to her days at finishing school, a dark place she didn't wish to return to. Mena reached over and laid a comforting hand on the young woman's forearm.

"One cake isn't something to fear. Even just having a little taste can brighten your day without creating any discomfort with your corset," she said, keeping her voice to a whisper.

"My mother…" the young woman breathed, shooting a fearful glance over at a sharp eyed looking older woman sitting across the room.

Mena's lips pressed together in a thin line. Mothers could be very controlling, even abusive, in the pursuit of a good marriage for their daughters.

"Later," Mena assured her, smiling secretively.

She would find a way to sneak some treats to this woman, and no meddling mothers could stop her.

Mena did her best to avoid staring at the duke through dinner, but she had attempted to look over at him covertly a few times, only to catch him watching her. It was unnerving, and exhilarating, if she were being honest.

And it didn't help that Mena was forced to wear her most hated of gowns, the pink ruffled nightmare she had previously loaned her dear friend Thalia the night she met her husband, Campbell Marlowe. It was a truly horrendous concoction of several tiers of alternating shades of bright pink, and covered in frills and flounces, lace and flowers. It looked like a dressmaker's monster, made from scraps. Mena's mother had adored it…five years ago.

All the other ladies wore sleek silhouettes with tasteful embellishments and glittering jewels. Mena wanted to sigh when she saw them all in their finery, none of it outdated like her own. Fashion has never been an interest of hers, and now that her mother was gone, Mena was relieved to have no need for a new gown.

Sadly, this left the pink one as her best option for a ball, though one could hardly call a small country house party a ball, and so it was the logical choice for any high society dance. Her mother had insisted on every detail of the deranged garment herself, much to Mena's chagrin.

As the couples began pairing off to float about the floor together, Mena perused the refreshments table. Once again, she had only picked at her dinner from worry over being seen gorging herself by the duke. She wanted him to notice her, as much as she wished to remain invisible. She was filled with contradictory emotions, and it was truly unsettling. Perhaps a visit to the stables in the morning would be good. She could spend some time with the animals, which always set her to rights.

Unfortunately, an ill-mannered toff sauntered up to the table as well and crowded Mena, pressing close enough for her to feel the heat from his body through her silk gown. He pretended to survey the offerings for a moment before turning to flash an oily smile in her direction. Mena suddenly wished that hoop skirts were still in fashion. A cage of whalebone did provide a good level of protection against this sort of bad behavior. Hat pins were also quite effective at deterring a forward gentleman, but alas one did not wear hats at a dance.

"Pardon me, but I find myself in need of a chair, and you are in my way," she said with a falsely bright smile, attempting to push past the gentleman.

But the toff, none other than Lord Beckwith, wouldn't let her escape so easily. He planted his feet firmly on the floor with one hand on the table by Mena's spine as he leaned in closer.

"Allow me to escort you, Miss Harvey-Morton."

His smooth aristocratic tones couldn't hide the predatory look in his dark eyes.

Mena stared him down, or up rather as she was shorter than he, calculating her options. There was no polite way for her to decline his offer. This was why she loathed society; propriety demanded women defer to men. Men who often couldn't be trusted.

"I can find my own seat, thank you my lord," she said flatly, chin raised, daring him to call out her faux pas.

Lord Beckwith looked displeased but stepped back slightly to allow Mena to pass by. As she did so though, he purposely brushed his hand against her upper arm, his skin sliding against her exposed flesh. Mena quickly pulled away and shot Lord Beckwith a disgusted look. He grinned at her, making her stomach roll.

She turned away and walked as confidently as she could across the room, letting the crowd of people wall her off from Lord Beckwith's advances. She walked all the way to the row of chairs sheltered by several tall ferns along the far wall. Mena sat in the one most hidden by foliage and worked on controlling her tumultuous emotions. Anger, fear, outrage, and worst of all, loneliness. She missed her friends, her animals, her usual life.

Looking down at her lap, Mena avoided looking at the other guests as they enjoyed themselves. She was isolated in misery and was working up to simply leave and head to her room when a pair of men's shoes came into view. She looked up, dreading who it might be, and was surprised to find the duke standing before her, hand extended. Mena stared at it in confusion, as though seeing a hand for the first time.

"May I have this dance, Miss Harvey-Morton?" he asked with a charmingly lopsided smile, hair burnished bronze in the lamplight.

Mena bobbed her head in an approximation of a nod and stood to place her hand in his. She could feel his heat through her glove and imagined an electrical current running between their fingers, a frisson of awareness that startled her with its intensity. She allowed the duke to lead her to the dance floor for a waltz.

Mena gasped as he pulled her close, one hand on her lower back in a possessive manner, the other holding hers so gently. She brought up her free hand to rest on his shoulder as they began to move to the music together. Blushing, Mena noticed that she could feel his muscles moving through the layers of his clothing.

The duke was not a soft man; his arms belied a strength that surprised and overwhelmed her. Mena was unused to being in such proximity to men like this, let alone being held by them. It was scandalous, really. For a society so hell bent on keeping women innocent, it was ridiculous what was allowed and what wasn't within the bounds of propriety. The duke was holding her far too close. Every time they turned she could feel the press of his legs through her skirts.

"Do you enjoy dancing, Mena?" he asked against her ear, his voice low enough to vibrate through her like thunder.

She shivered deliciously and was mortified to think that he might have felt it too. Mena looked up at him, studying his eyes.

"I do not enjoy anything related to crowds," she admitted ruefully. "This sort of thing is my idea of a nightmare."

The duke frowned, seeming concerned, and then looked off over her head. Before she realized what was happening, he was leading her toward the terrace doors, thrown open to the night. Mena laughed nervously as he twirled her around and out the door. They came to a stop in the cooler air, and the sound of crickets in the distant fields settled upon them.

"Is this better?" the duke asked, releasing his hold on her, and turning to rest his forearms on the terrace wall that overlooked the geometric garden below.

The fountain could be heard gurgling somewhere nearby, but it was too dark to see anything.

"Yes, thank you," Mena replied, pressing her hands to her warm cheeks. "I'm not used to this sort of thing. I mostly avoid society."

The duke turned around, leaning back against the railing, and stuck his hands in his trouser pockets. He cocked his head slightly as he regarded her.

"Why is that?"

Mena shifted awkwardly.

"I suppose big groups of people make me nervous," she sighed, looking up at the brilliant moon. "Always have."

"So, you decided to brave the fray for a chance at winning my hand despite this fear, dear lady?" he said.

Was he flirting with her? The thought of a duke flirting with her sent a quiver down her spine.

"What?" she squeaked, voice cracking badly, forcing her to clear her throat with a cough.

He grinned at her, practically blinding her with the brilliance of his smile. The man was dangerous. And arrogant, as though he expected all women to fall for him with ease.

"Ah yes, you've caught me out, your grace," Mena laughed nervously.

"Garrett, remember?" he said softly, his dark eyes holding some emotion she couldn't name.

"My apologies. Garrett," she said with a coy smile, loving the feeling of his name on her tongue. "Tell me, have you found your match yet?"

"My match?" he repeated, looking off through the doors into the ballroom. "I don't know. How does one select a bride? I wouldn't know where to begin."

Mena considered that.

"I suppose you look for someone who you could stand seeing every day for the rest of your life."

The duke barked out a laugh.

"That sounds simple enough," he said.

"As a duke with money—and I know that it's vulgar to comment on it, but alas I am not very good at following society's rules—you don't need a bride with money or a flashy title. So that leaves you with the next important thing, personality. Do any of them," she indicated the ballroom with her hand, "have qualities you find attractive?"

Garrett lifted a brow.

"They are all beautiful, but I don't know if I could spend the rest of my life talking to any of them," he admitted, turning serious.

"To be fair, young ladies are not encouraged to be interesting. We are to show no interest in anything important, most especially politics." She grimaced. "My own mother used to rip books out of my hands and burn them."

"Why would she do that?" he asked with interest.

Mena shrugged, affecting nonchalance even as the memory still ached.

"Because it was interfering with my time for gossip and gowns. She despaired of me never marrying."

"So, her last attempt is throwing you in the path of a duke?"

If he meant that as a joke, Mena didn't laugh. She felt the familiar sting of anger and guilt that arose whenever she thought about her mother.

"No, actually. I came here because my father asked me to. He needed someone on his arm, and besides, my mother died several years ago," she said flatly, carefully unemotional.

"I'm sorry," Garrett said, his eyes held not a hint of pity, for which she was grateful.

"Don't be," she shook her head. "It was a relief, though I know that sentiment should be shocking."

"I would be the last person who should judge you for having such feelings," he said, and turned back to the garden, frowning off into the fathomless distance. After a moment he spoke again, voice low. "My father was not a kind man."

Mena moved to stand beside Garrett, resting her arms on the wall close to his.

"You don't have to tell me anything, Garrett," she said softly.

He turned slightly to look at her out of the corner of his eye.

"I know," he said with a small smile.

They stood like that, side by side, arms occasionally brushing against each other until the music ended. Then several couples came out for some air, breaking the spell of intimacy that had woven around them. They looked at each other, both seeming to feel the same sting of the moment ending.

Mena rested a hand on Garrett's arm for a moment, intending it as a friendly gesture. But the sensation of touching him so boldly felt decidedly more than friendly; something altogether different. She quickly pulled her hand back, a fierce blush burning her cheeks. She took a step back, creating more space between them.

"I think I should be getting to bed. I'm not usually up so late," she explained.

Flicking a glance at the others on the terrace, Mena dipped into a shallow curtsy and fled without looking at Garrett again, avoiding his eyes and their intensity. She was a fool for spending any time with such a man, let alone allowing the intrusion of ridiculous thoughts. Thoughts like kissing the duke.

Mena would rather die than admit to her attraction to him. Surely the duke saw her as all others did: a plain woman who was far too timid and boring to spend any time thinking about, let alone kissing. He would surely be horrified and embarrassed by the turn of her thoughts.

"Good night," he called after her, but Mena didn't break stride to acknowledge his farewell.

Seven

arrett had not slept well. Having houseguests was awkward at the best of times, but a house full of eager young women all vying for his attention was so much worse. He couldn't walk around his own house in peace without running into an eager young lady vying to show off her many charms and talents.

And then there was the problem of Miss Philomena Harvey-Morton. Claire had told him what he had already deduced, that she was socially a nobody, a plain brown-haired woman who hated social gatherings, with no money and no connections. Her father had been invited to lend the weekend an air of respectability, given the purpose of the entire affair.

Despite all that, there was something about Miss Harvey-Morton that kept his thoughts circling back to her, to every hint of emotion he caught when her stoic mask slipped, to her unconventional freshness, and the ease with which he could simply be himself with her. Relaxed in a way that was quite unexpected.

It was strange and surprising, and absolutely something he had to avoid. Garrett needed to keep his wits about him so he could get through his weekend and continue to live his uncomplicated life without any entanglements. Miss Harvey-Morton was a complication.

The morning after the dancing was a wash-out, with rain steadily hammering down upon anyone unfortunate enough to go outside. Being that it was getting on toward autumn, the air held a chill as well.

Claire attempted to steer people toward various pursuits to keep them busy. Some were sent to the library, others to the billiard room, but most of the young ladies had chosen to sit in the parlor to do some needlework or play a game of whist to while away the long afternoon. It seemed the sexes were determined to avoid each other, and Garrett wasn't going to break with the mood of the house. He gleefully took the opportunity to sneak outside for some fresh, albeit damp, air.

Using the front door, Garrett hurried past the butler, who attempted to hand him an umbrella. But Garrett didn't stop; he bounded down the front steps and along the drive toward the stables, quickly getting soaked by the pouring rain. He was coming around the side of the stables when he collided with another person.

"Apologies," he exclaimed, reaching out to steady them.

It was Miss Harvey-Morton, completely wet through. She stared up at him owlishly, her lips pressed so tightly together they seemed to disappear. Her dark hair hung limply down to her waist, dripping. A shiver ran through her, and she began rubbing her arms for warmth.

"My God, Mena, how long have you been out in the rain? We should get you inside," Garrett said with concern.

The woman might not be completely sane, running around in the rain alone and without a coat or umbrella. Some protective instinct drove him to want to rescue her, though he doubted she was the type to appreciate that sentiment much. She continued to stare at him without answering, and Garrett began looking around for somewhere to take her. A fire and some blankets couldn't be found in the stables, and Garrett didn't want to return to the house. Then he remembered the estate cottage would be empty, since Campbell and his bride had moved into their new home in the village.

He offered her his most reassuring smile.

"Let's go get you warm and dry, shall we?" he asked as he took her arm, tucked it into his elbow, and began walking swiftly with her through the rain toward the cottage.

A thin path through the woods led to an adorable English thatched cottage covered in climbing roses. It had been Campbell's home for years, but now he would be living in the village with his new bride, leaving the cottage empty. It wasn't far to walk, and soon Garrett was leading Mena up the front steps to the cottage door and out of the rain.

Once the door was shut behind them, Garrett found an old hand stitched quilt draped over the back of the settee. The dowager duchess had spent much of her time hidden away here at the cottage avoiding her husband, and this quilt was just one of many that she had painstakingly worked on over the years. Garrett shook his head to clear away the cobwebs of old memories, and gently tucked the blanket around Mena's shoulders.

"Thank you," she murmured, and wiped at her face to dry it.

She met his eyes again, black lashes spiked with rain, and seemed to take a deep fortifying breath before speaking.

"I was taking a walk when the rain grew worse. I had almost made it back when you found me. I walk alone often, though my dog used to accompany me before he grew too old. Staying inside all day makes me stir-crazy. I just needed some air."

"I had the same thought, but only made it to the stables," he smiled. "You must have had an early start."

Mena looked down at her muddy hem and grimaced.

"I did. I find it difficult to sleep in someone else's bed."

Garrett swallowed a laugh as her cheeks blushed bright pink as she apparently realized what she had just said, her eyes wide with horror.

"You know what I meant," Mena scowled at him, though her lips twitched with suppressed humor.

Garrett was still, his mind racing through images of Mena naked and tangled in his sheets, her mahogany hair trailing across his chest as he held her lush body. She must have read something in his expression because she turned serious, watching him with that carefully blank expression, hiding herself.

Garrett didn't want her to hide from him. He took the ends of the blanket Mena had wrapped around her, and gently began to dry her hair. She stood very still, allowing him the privilege as she watched him with wide eyes.

* * *

His face was mere inches from hers, his sky-blue eyes burning her with their intensity. Mena simply stared back, helpless with the anticipation that was building between them, like an electric current that drew them together. Then finally, blessedly, his mouth slowly descended upon hers, claiming her lips in a sweet kiss. The barest caress of his mouth on hers. She breathed in his scent, all warm soap and rich coffee.

Mena's eyes fluttered closed, and she leaned into Garrett's strength, allowing him to support her as her legs felt a bit wobbly.

One of his large hands was on her lower back, possessively holding her against the length of his hard body as he proceeded to kiss her more thoroughly. His free arm braced against the door at her back, cocooning Mena in his warmth. Their kiss grew in intensity with each breath as their lips pressed and molded each other's.

The slide of his skin on her, the rush of his breath, so close, was astonishing. The moment seemed to stand apart from reality, fragile and intimate and timeless. Mena could feel her pulse thumping in her chest and she burned with need as she clung to Garrett, reveling in this kiss. Her first kiss.

She whimpered, desperate to get closer, and dropped her hold on the blanket, which slid down to puddle on the floor around their feet. Her arms went up around his neck, inadvertently pushing her breasts into his solid chest. She was a being of pure need. Her fingers skimmed the edge of his starched collar, feeling the satin softness of those rakish golden curls.

He groaned, broke the kiss, much to Mena's frustration, and held still, pressing his forehead to hers as their harsh breathing filled the silence of the house. Their eyes held, and Mena was undone by the intimacy of this moment. She had never experienced anything comparable, having never been so much as flirted with before.

Logically she knew better than to fall in love with a duke, but her heart was a ridiculous thing that had its own ideas. She pulled away with a sigh and attempted to look confident. Garrett's eyes were dark with desire. He took a slow, deep breath, and stepped back.

"Well," she said softly, knowing that she looked absolutely awful from the rain and…well, her wardrobe.

Suddenly she wished for a gown other than the worn gray cotton one she had donned earlier. She wanted to look alluring, beautiful, enticing. What was wrong with her? She needed to cool down and think logically.

"Why did you kiss me?" she asked, glad that her voice was steady.

"I don't know," he admitted, looking chagrined. "I apologize for...well, to put it badly, compromising your virtue."

His smile was lopsided and hopeful, and he looked absurdly boyish with his hair flopping across his brow. A startled laugh escaped her, easing the tension between them and erasing her discomfort. She liked him.

"That's ridiculous," Mena laughed. "My virtue is covered in dust and set up on a high shelf to wither away."

"It still exists," he pointed out.

"My virtue is of no concern to anyone, except perhaps my father," she grimaced at the thought of him discovering them like this.

He would enthusiastically frog march them to the altar.

"Well, it is of concern to me," the duke said firmly.

Mena scoffed.

"There is no need, really. I am not here to catch a husband. You needn't concern yourself. This was a... lovely mistake, and nothing needs to come from this," she assured him. "Besides, I am twenty-seven and can do as I like."

Garrett considered this and nodded slowly.

"To be fair, I am twenty-nine and cannot do as I like all of the time. Can I be honest with you and admit that I'm not here to catch a bride either?" he admitted, looking guilty.

Mena's brow crinkled in confusion.

"Is that not what this weekend is about? Why is your home filled with eligible women if not for you to choose one as a wife?"

"It's a ridiculous story, I assure you. But I've been avoiding marriage for years and I'm not about to end up leg shackled now."

"Is your sister attempting to force your hand?" she asked.

"Yes, but she's not too bothersome about it. Every year she gives me a lecture about duty, but her heart isn't truly in it."

"Ah, this is the party you were supposed to throw for Mr. Marlow, is that right?" she asked, realizing the truth of it.

Garrett looked surprised, but nodded.

"Thalia told me about it, but I didn't know that all this was all still for him," she explained. "It was good of you to help your friend."

"I couldn't just cancel at the last minute with no explanation. Besides, the ladies my sister invited were told that I was hunting a bride. I didn't want to leave her looking foolish," the duke said with a grimace. "Do you know Thalia well? I'm surprised we have never met before."

"She has been a close friend for years. But I do my best to avoid introductions," she laughed. "Campbell was a fool to think that money could buy happiness," she added.

"It seems to have all worked out in the end," Garrett smiled.

Mena nodded, feeling envy stirring, which was absurd and left her feeling ashamed. She should be happy for her friend, not jealous because she had no love of her own.

"Yes, it has," she agreed.

They stood together awkwardly for a moment while Mena dried herself off as best she could. Garrett watched her, hands in his pockets, still standing close enough for his warmth to permeate her damp clothing. Mena wanted to squirm under the scrutiny.

"Would you like me to start a fire for you? You were so cold before," he asked, apparently just remembering his earlier intention.

Mena shook her head as she finished drying herself.

"We should be getting back. I know you will be greatly missed," she said, and held the blanket out to Garrett.

"I should go and have a carriage sent back for you."

"No! That wouldn't be a good idea," Mena said. "This never happened."

** * **

Garrett stared at her, his brain relieved that she didn't intend to try and trick him into marriage. Yet somehow, he also felt disappointed.

"You're right, of course."

Mena nodded and turned to open the door.

"The rain has slowed down significantly," she observed, and looked back at him over her shoulder with a smile.

"How fortuitous," he forced himself to say cheerfully.

Garrett walked Mena back to the house in companionable silence, both consumed by their private thoughts. Once back at the main house, he was careful to allow Mena to walk in alone, so no one would suspect they had been alone together. Once she was safely inside, he walked around to another door, slipping in without notice.

He made it up to his rooms without bumping into anyone, and once he was behind his own locked door, Garrett stripped off his jacket and waistcoat, throwing them in a soggy heap on the floor. He crossed the room to his bed and sat down on the pristine counterpane to remove his boots.

As he was unbuttoning his wet shirt, and peeling the now translucent fabric from his skin, Garrett's mind was captivated by Mena and her passionate response to his kiss. No one would have suspected such a wanton nature lay just beneath that stoic surface she so carefully maintained. The woman was a walking contradiction, endlessly fascinating, and Garrett needed to stay the hell away from her.

He was sinking fast, and needed to save himself, lest he find himself leg shackled to a village virgin. From now on he would endeavor to avoid her at all costs. Unfortunately, the sample he'd experienced of her charms only left him wanting more, and he couldn't stop thinking about kissing her again, tasting her, hearing her moan his name.

Christ, he was in trouble.

Chapter

Eight

After having successfully avoided the duke for the remainder of the day, Mena knew she would be forced to take part in the activities on the next. Thankfully it was a picnic luncheon, which meant she could enjoy the sunshine and excellent food.

It was Sunday, and those who were inclined went to church service in the morning, while the others had kept busy touring the extensive portrait gallery, led by Lady Claire, while the rain fell. Mena had been busy assisting her father with the church service in town, but now she was back and needed to face the duke, and the entire retinue of house guests.

Because of the rain the river was swollen and moving fast, so Lady Claire had decided to hold the picnic in one of the estate follies. Several guests elected to be driven by carriage to the folly, but Mena preferred to walk, mostly so she could arrive late and thereby shave off some time she was expected to endure the general assembly.

Upon leaving her room after changing from her church gown into a simpler faded lavender frock sprigged with tiny white flowers, Mena walked carefully to avoid bumping into anyone, especially the duke. After that kiss, she wasn't sure how she could ever look him in the eye again. She wore her most flattering dress, but she was not angling for the duke's hand, and was absolutely not trying to get him to look at her. Well, perhaps she did want him to find her attractive, but that didn't mean anything.

Downstairs in the foyer it was chaos, with a riot of colorful day dresses and so many people talking at once. Mena wanted to cover her ears but forced herself to remain calm. She kept to the wall, so as to avoid getting shoved or trampled, and made her way to the front door.

The butler hastened to open the door when she approached, but several ladies assumed their carriage had arrived and it was a crush to get out the door. Mena cried out in surprise as she was practically lifted and pushed along with the crowd. It was like being caught in a swift current and taken out to sea.

The noon sun was finally breaking free from the clouds, but the road had numerous puddles waiting to snag a carriage wheel or ruin someone's stockings. Once she was able to separate herself from the crowd, Mena put some distance between herself and the crowd milling about on the front steps. She saw her father, who waved to her before claiming a horse from an approaching footman. He swung into the saddle with surprising agility and trotted over.

"Are you going to ride to the folly, Philomena?" he asked, frowning down at her.

"No, I could use the walk. And the gardens are quite lovely," she replied, shielding her eyes from the sun as she craned her neck to look up at her father.

"Alright, but do hurry along please. I think I am doing well with the duke and could use your presence. And for heaven's sake, put on your bonnet."

Mena's jaw clenched. She maintained a bland expression, but it wasn't easy.

"I will."

Sir Harvey-Morton nodded and rode off on his borrowed mare. Three carriages had arrived and the guests were all climbing in, with plenty of giggling to be had. At a distance, Mena followed along behind the carriages as they drove away. She knew where the folly was located, thanks to her maid, and wasn't concerned when the carriages quickly disappeared around a turn. The silence was welcome, and Mena intended to enjoy it for as long as possible.

She swung her straw bonnet from its white satin ribbons as she walked along the path, which was lined with neatly trimmed hedges. She intended to don the hat at the last possible minute, as it was lovely feeling the sun on her face and the gentle breeze in her hair, which was tightly braided and coiled again by her borrowed ladies maid.

The sound of horse hooves came up behind her, and she turned to see who it was. Of course, she groaned quietly. The duke slowed beside her, and damn him for looking glorious in his green riding suit and snow white neckcloth. His golden hair fell perfectly over his forehead, giving him a purposely tousled look. How did he do that? Mena twisted her fingers together nervously.

"Hello," she said, cringing as she heard the unnaturally high pitch of her voice.

"Hello yourself. Why are you walking? The puddles are a hazard," he replied, frowning.

"I think I can be trusted to avoid puddles thank you very much," Mena scowled, chin up. "I've kept myself alive thus far."

A low chuckle made her stomach flip. Garrett's laugh was absurdly sensual, sending a hot shiver down her spine, pooling heat between her legs. *Damn him*, she silently cursed.

"I don't doubt that. You are quite a stubborn person," he casually remarked.

Mena's jaw dropped open.

"That's not true!" she exclaimed, outraged. "I believe that I am, in fact, far too acquiescent."

Garrett looked skeptical, but didn't argue. His eyes sparkled with a mischievous glint.

"Regardless, I intend to walk to the folly. Please go on ahead, or people will see us alone together and…get ideas," she finished with a blush.

She cast Garrett a sidelong look and found him watching her with an odd expression. But he nodded after a moment.

"Enjoy your walk," he called as he rode off leaving Mena on her own.

She was almost sorry that she'd sent him off—almost. The silence left in the wake of the chaotic party heading off was calming. She kicked at a stone on the path as she walked, keeping her steps slow to stretch out the time.

Sadly, it was a rather short walk, and Mena was soon within earshot of the party again, the laughter and gossip hitting her ears before she could even see the revelers. She sighed, wishing she could just keep walking and go home. But alas, that would worry her father. She continued on, letting her feet carry her toward the inevitably awful situation. She paused to settle her bonnet on her head, tying the white ribbon firmly beneath her chin.

The folly was built to look like a miniature Parthenon, but open in the center to allow for tables to be set up. All around the folly were fragrant late summer flower beds blooming with a riot of colors. Nearby the river flowed, willows dangling their long branches into the water.

Despite the earlier rain, the ground must have already dried, for several large blankets had been spread out and footmen were busy unpacking baskets of food and drinks for the guests who were artfully lounging. There was a spot available next to Lady Claire, but Mena sensed that sitting by her would lead to more attention, which she was trying to avoid. Though perhaps it would be perfect, and Lady Claire would do all the heavy lifting when it came to conversation. Mena decided to gamble on it, and sat down carefully, tucking her skirts in around her legs.

"How lovely to have a chance to sit by you, Miss Harvey-Morton," Lady Claire said, by all accounts seeming genuine in her pleasure.

Mena wasn't sure what to say to that.

"Umm, yes well…" she mumbled, and was thankfully interrupted by another lady who rushed to tell Lady Claire how much she admired her dress.

Mena sat stiffly and tried to avoid eye contact with anyone, lest she encourage conversation. The sound of her father's enthusiastic guffaws grated on her frayed nerves. The male members of the picnic group mostly lounged on the blankets, leaning on elbows or lying completely flat to relax. The older guests, her father included, were provided little wooden folding chairs to assist them in standing once lunch had been eaten. Mena studiously ignored the conversation flowing from that side of the picnic blanket, and instead trained her attention on the ladies beside her.

"…and her dress was a most horrid shade of yellow, I must divulge. Her skin looked quite sallow in the lamplight…"

Soft tuts and murmurs followed these hushed bits of gossip. It was exceedingly dull and disappointing. Couldn't ladies talk of anything interesting when in private? The men wouldn't notice if they all suddenly broke into a serious study of political economy, for example. Mena knew what would happen if she attempted to broach such topics though, having a vast schooling experience to call upon. It was futile, at best, and could accidentally create enemies, at worst. She longed for a picnic with her friends, who were always ready to discuss more serious topics—things that actually mattered.

She turned away, toward the sound of water. The river was close by, she could smell its earthiness and the stands of willows and rushes nearby. The air held a touch of crispness, heralding the change of seasons, and the sun felt glorious on her face. Mena tipped her head back slightly, allowing more of her face to be loved by the sun, wishing she could remove her ridiculous straw hat. Her scalp already felt pinched by the artful arrangement of hair she'd been forced to sport, not to mention the chafing caused by her straw hat. Mena longed to remove it, but resisted.

"Miss Harvey-Morton?"

Mena jerked in surprise at hearing her name. Her head swiveled to find three ladies patiently waiting for her to speak. Mena blinked at them, wracking her brain for a response that wouldn't leave her looking odd.

"We were saying, Miss Harvey-Morton," Lady Claire smiled. "That we have boats available for those who would enjoy a little ride on the water after lunch."

"That sounds lovely," Mena said woodenly, and cleared her throat.

Lady Claire's smile grew wider, and she clapped her hands together.

"Wonderful," she said.

Suddenly a teacup and saucer appeared in the air between them, and Mena turned to find a footman there. Lady Claire accepted the cup, and a second one was handed to Mena. Plates of finger sandwiches, tarts, and pies were placed on the blankets, and glasses of lemonade were handed out as well.

Every detail had been considered. Small, low tables had been put in convenient places nearby so one wasn't forced to juggle too many items and ruin the enjoyment of the meal. Mena happily tucked into the delicious food, avoiding further conversation.

This was a very different type of picnic luncheon than she would have with her friends. They always had simple fare, and simply enjoyed the moment outside together. What would they think of this fancy affair? Mena could imagine Clementine referring to the gathering as stuffy. She was not the sort to be satisfied by all this sitting around and wasting time, when instead she could be out trying to improve society.

At least the thought of her friends helped ease Mena's discomfort here amongst the glittering ladies of the ton.

Unfortunately, after eating, she came to find out that she had accidentally agreed to go for a ride in one of the little dinghies that waited by the edge of the river. Lady Claire beamed as she paired Mena off with Lord Beckwith. Of course. Mena bit the inside of her cheek to keep from screaming in frustration. She did not have the patience for that man today.

Mena peered skeptically at the river sluggishly flowing by. Suddenly, as though conjured by her deepest desires, the duke appeared.

"How is it that you've never gone boating?" Garrett asked with a laugh.

In the sunlight he looked glorious, looking at her with a devilish glint in his blue eyes. Mena resisted the impulse to kiss him. No more kissing.

"How do you know I've never been boating?" she demanded tartly.

He laughed, and said, "I can see how nervous you are," as he extended a hand to her.

Mena took his hand without a second thought, placing her trust in this man whom she barely knew. Lord Beckwith looked on in exasperation as he watched the duke handily maneuver Mena into his own watercraft. One did not refuse a duke, so with a deep bow, the other man made himself scarce.

And they were off, leaving the other guests behind as the river eased them along. Mena laughed with delight, but clutched the sides of the boat, her knuckles white. The duke studied her face for a moment, and frowned.

"You really are afraid," he said, rather than asked.

Mena was tempted to lie.

"I find this sensation incredibly overwhelming…and frightening," she admitted.

The duke's expression grew very serious, and he rowed faster, angling the boat toward shore. The movement of his powerful arms and chest was incredibly distracting, his jacket stretching over his muscles with each movement. Mena told herself that her staring was just to cure her fear; it was a useful distraction and nothing else.

The boat soon bumped against the shore, and the duke leaped out with the grace of a panther to tie it to a nearby tree. Mena's fingers clung to the wooden sides of the boat, her eyes tracking his movements, heart hammering. Garrettcame back swiftly and helped her out onto the firm ground.

Mena stumbled, her knees weak from nerves and the rocking of the boat, falling against the duke's strong body. She tipped her head back, meeting his eyes.

"I don't think I like boating," she managed before noticing her hands splayed across his broad chest and proceeding to blush furiously.

Mena snatched her hands away, but the duke didn't release her right away.

"I apologize, Mena," he said softly, his eyes serious and searching. "If I had known how it would affect you, I never would have put you in the boat."

Mena was taken aback. A duke was apologizing to her, for causing her distress. For as long as she could remember, her emotional state was her problem and was something to be covered up and apologized for. No one had ever made her feel like this burden wasn't her fault, or due to her poor behavior or lack of control, but instead something that could be faced and handled. She felt less alone, and predictably her eyes welled up with tears. Blast.

Nine

Garrett was horrified to see tears gathering in Mena's eyes. He couldn't stand seeing women cry, it always made him so helpless—an uncharacteristic emotion, due to his insistence on never being in that position, if he could help it. But at this moment he didn't feel helpless or uncomfortable. He felt something else…something difficult to name. He reached up and used the pad of his thumb to wipe a tear away as it slid down her cheek, feeling a warm tenderness expanding in his chest.

They stood like that for an eternity, staring at each other as though seeing each other for the first time. Garrett was lost in her rich coffee-colored eyes, fringed with thick black lashes. A golden sprinkle of freckles graced the delicate bridge of her nose, almost invisible unless one made a study of her countenance. From the gossip circulating the party, there were those who thought her to be plain—even Garrett had thought so—but now…she was alluring. Her full lips parted in surprise as his thumb swept across her skin.

Garrett's dreams had been filled with her. It was unnerving how much he had thought about her in the past two days. She was a stranger, a nobody, an uncultured country lass, and Garrett was determined not to end up betrothed after this weekend. And yet it seemed that fate conspired to throw him and Mena together.

He was about to kiss her again. The tension of the moment felt as fragile as a soap bubble.

Suddenly the moment was broken by the sound of an approaching carriage. Mena stepped back, away from him. Why that tore at him, Garrett was unsure. But he wanted to keep her near.

They had not gone far down the river before coming ashore, and a carriage road for pleasure drives wound around the river as well. It sounded like the servants decided to save the duke from an unwanted marriage by rescuing him from being alone with a female. Garrett would normally have been grateful, but curiously felt annoyed instead. Soon enough a footman appeared to assist them back to the estate house.

"John, please escort Miss Harvey-Morton back to the main house. I shall row the dinghy back to the boathouse," Garrett said, trying to sound normal when he felt somewhat…unsettled.

Mena watched him for a moment before turning toward the path to the road, and the waiting carriage. She held her head high, shoulders stiffly erect, like a schoolmarm. But something about her seemed so vulnerable. Why hadn't Garrett noticed it before? Mena's attempts at cloaking herself in dignity made it all the more obvious how tumultuous her existence was. The way she had reacted to the boat, her self-imposed social isolation… Mena was a woman full of fears and traumas. Garrett knew better than to get involved, to pry into her affairs, but he couldn't help his interest.

After Mena and the footman had left, Garrett climbed back into the boat. The work of rowing the little boat against the stream was welcome, allowing Garrett to settle into a rhythm of physical exertion sure to cure his restless thoughts. Except that it didn't. When he got the boat back to the dock and tied it off, he still felt unsettled.

The picnic party had moved on, returning to the house for a rest or a game of croquet on the lawn. The plates, glasses, and blankets were efficiently packed up by the footmen and returned to the baskets they'd arrived in. A groom noticed Garrett watching the progress and brought over the enormous black stallion the duke preferred to ride while in the country.

Garrett accepted the reins and nodded to the groom. He stroked the horse's long velvety nose. Perhaps a ride would help. At the very least it would provide some much-needed space from his guests. Garrett couldn't handle forcing a smile to his face as he discussed the latest fashions and weather with tittering ladies just now. Or ever, if possible.

He hooked a boot into one of the stirrups and swung up into the saddle. The horse tossed its tail, but stood solidly waiting for a command. Garrett patted the horse's neck and then dug his heels in. The wind in his hair felt good. Freeing. If only he could keep going and not ever go back.

Oddly that sentiment wasn't confined to simply running away from his guests, but also from his life and responsibilities. He had never really felt that way before. Yes, he was disinterested in his role, but never before had he chafed so much at the pressure.

Garrett raced along at a gallop, seeing the blur of trees and fields turned golden in the afternoon light. It was all his land. Why should anyone think him qualified to control the lives of so many?

Was he having a bit of a life crisis?

He circled back around to the barn, and brushed out the horse himself. After providing fresh hay and water, Garrett finally returned to the house for a bath. Submerged in the hot water, he washed away the sweat and grime and allowed himself to temporarily get lost in his thoughts.

* * *

Dinner was agony. Garrett stole glances at Mena, trying to determine her mood. But she was stoic as ever, eating sparingly. Several times the Countess of Crenshaw tried to engage him in conversation, but he couldn't pay attention and she soon gave up.

After, in the parlor, more agony. A chess game was going on, and two card tables. Others sat by the open terrace doors enjoying the cool evening air, discussing poetry. Garrett despised these sorts of discussions, but Mena was sitting nearby, and he was inexplicably drawn to her, wanting to be close.

"Lovely to have you join us, your grace," Lady Violetta simpered. "We were discussing Robert Browning."

"Ah yes, well don't let me interrupt the flow of dialogue," Garrett said with an easy smile.

The ladies all practically swooned at this and seemed quite pleased. Blessedly the conversation progressed to other poets and Garrett was not pressed to prove he knew who the fuck Tennyson was.

This lasted for an hour before everyone grew tired of the subject, and many wandered off to bed. One of the card games continued, and some guests lingered by the empty fireplace and spoke quietly.

Finally, Garrett had a chance to speak with Mena. She sat in the shadowed corner of the room, almost out on the terrace. In the room, but isolated from it. How fitting. Garrett leaned against the wall, hands in his pockets casually.

"You look much improved from this afternoon. Are you feeling better?" he asked.

Mena's head turned, and she regarded him steadily.

"Much better, thank you," she murmured.

"So, you don't enjoy boating, nor riding it seems. You did not participate in the poetry discourse. I give up, Miss Harvey-Morton. What is your passion?"

Her brown eyes widened in surprise.

"You want to know about my passions?" she asked in a shyly flirtatious tone.

Garrett nodded slowly, enjoying the color creeping into her cheeks. She shifted, and turned her gaze out into the dark garden. She looked around nervously, ensuring they were truly alone. After a few minutes of silent thought, she finally spoke.

"When I attended finishing school, I thought I was finally escaping my mother's machinations. She was quite controlling, you see. But I found it was just as bad there as it was at home."

She swallowed, staring blindly out into the dark garden.

"I met another girl named Ashely, and life became a little more bearable…but one day she was forced to leave. We've kept in touch though, and she is finally happy. I'm glad for her, but I know many other women are stuck right now in terrible circumstances and…I just want to be able to help them. So that's my passion, your grace. Helping other women."

Garrett looked at her, feeling something difficult to name expand within him. It was a strange amalgamation of respect and envy. What could he say of himself and his own pursuits? Nothing so heroic as what this diminutive woman had just shared, baring her soul to him. He knew it was special that she had opened up as she had.

He lamented shirking the many responsibilities belonging to the title he held, managing to offload most of the work running the estate to others, like Campbell who had—until recently—been in complete control of the estate operations. Garrett was suddenly struck with guilt, for not being the man he should have been all these years for those who depended on him. This lovely young woman was making him question everything about the way he had lived his life up until now.

"That is admirable, Mena. What does your father have to say about this pursuit?"

She laughed, but her tone was laced with bitterness.

"For a long time, my father didn't seem to care what I did with my life. It has been extremely refreshing…up until now."

She turned and leveled a frustrated look at Garrett.

"Fathers tend to draw the line at eligible dukes looking for a wife."

He strove for a light tone, perhaps even to elicit a laugh from her. Even as those words made his throat constrict.

"It is most annoying," she replied with a small curve of her lips. "I was finally feeling settled in myself. Certain of things. And now…"

She stopped, looking up at him with an anxious expression as if she had said too much, revealed herself. Garrett stilled. He understood, feeling mixed up and confused himself. She cleared her throat and looked down at her hands.

"So, for now I work at the orphanage in the village, and try to aid other women when I can."

Garrett's heart squeezed painfully in his chest. He thought to share something of himself with her, but couldn't summon the words. His instinct, as usual, was to try and lighten the mood.

"Did you enjoy your reading the other night?"

That startled a genuine laugh from her, and some of the tension eased from Garrett's chest at the sound.

"Yes, it was most illuminating."

"Come to the library with me. I might have a suggestion for your next conquest."

He wiggled his eyebrows playfully at her, and tilted his head in invitation toward the parlor door. Mena hesitated, thinking it over, but eventually nodded and stood to follow. Garrett led the way across the room, where only a few guests remained, and out to the hall. Hopefully no one would notice their leaving. They walked in silence to the library.

"Ah, here it is," Garrett said, extracting a black leather-bound volume from the shelf near the fireplace.

Mena padded across the carpet to stand beside him; her skirts rustled as she moved. Reaching out to take the book, her fingers brushed against his and Garrett felt a shock of awareness at the touch of her bare skin. Mena met his eyes, a look of naked yearning in her gaze.

Without thinking, Garrett reached for her.

Ten

Mena's head spun as the duke pulled her close, pressing her against the steel of his form. His muscles bunched under her fingers as her hands went up to clutch his shoulders for balance. The world was turned onto its head. The duke stared down at her, his expression bemused.

"Bloody hell," he murmured, his voice more of a growl.

His large hand cupped her jaw as his head dipped down to kiss her. Her. Miss Philomena Harvey-Morton, a mere vicar's daughter, was being kissed by a handsome duke. Again.

The very duke that ladies were competing over, whispering about, and hoping to ensnare in marriage. And he was kissing Mena like she was irresistible. His heat warmed her, and she shamelessly pressed against him. The rough pad of his thumb rested by the corner of her mouth as his lips molded over hers.

The duke's lips were achingly gentle as he claimed hers, teasing her. Mena let out a helpless moan as she slid her hands up into his silken hair. He growled in response, the sensation pooling a heat low in her belly. She rubbed against him like a cat, trying to soothe the ache that was driving her wild. Garrett responded by licking at the seam of her lips, demanding entry. His other hand, braced against her lower back, slid down to cup her backside, pulling her hips against his own. He used his other hand to tilt her head back and deepen the kiss, delving inside her mouth, tasting her, thrusting inside her.

Mena whimpered and reflexively curled her fingers into his hair, tugging the thick locks, scraping her nails gently against his scalp. This seemed to snap the remaining threads of his control, for the next thing she knew, the duke picked her up easily and set her on the edge of the desk, stepping between her thighs. The feel of a man between her legs, so close to her, was shocking but it felt so right. By instinct she cradled him there, holding him close with her legs hooked around his hips.

She kissed him back, tentatively exploring his mouth with her tongue. The duke moaned encouragingly, and began tugging at her bodice, seeking to reveal more of her body to his ministrations.

Never in her wildest dreams had Mena imagined anything so erotic. It was as though she had fallen through a magic mirror into a very different world. One in which she was a wanton siren, someone who made men shudder with need. What delicious sorcery was this?

This could be her one opportunity to experience pleasure in a man's arms. She was not a beauty who attracted a string of suitors and would likely die an old maid. It was a ridiculous, idiotic idea, but once it popped into her mind, she was unable to shake it off. This was her chance, and she was going to take it. She was going to enjoy every moment. Whatever this man wanted to give, she would take gladly. The memory of this moment would sustain her for years in her cold lonely bed, living out her years as a spinster.

Mena huffed in frustration as she tried to get closer, to feel more. She was pure sensation, logic banished. She was a being entirely made of need, and she couldn't find satisfaction.

"Easy, love," he murmured in her ear, his hot breath fanning her skin as his mouth wandered along her jawline and down her throat, finding new places that made her toes curl.

"You make me feel so good," Mena sighed, completely undone by his touch.

Somehow, she had lost the ability to feel shame, and lived only for the sensations she was experiencing. The duke smiled against her skin and lapped at the hollow at the base of her throat. He kissed his way along the top edge of her gown, which was loosened due to his sly fingers.

Mena was too lost in the moment to feel anything but building excitement and anticipation as he eased her gown down to expose her breasts. She looked up into his eyes, assessing his reaction as he gazed upon her, and saw only hunger and desire in his expression. Then he leaned down and took one rosy nipple in his mouth, igniting a fire inside her that caused her to cry out. The duke raised his head long enough to press a kiss to her lips, before returning to his task, wringing pleasure from her body in a way she had never imagined before.

Mena clamped her lips together, trying to stay quiet as she endured the erotic assault, fingers tangled in his hair to hold him there. The rough bristles of his evening beard added to the bonfire of desire she felt, threatening to burn her to a crisp on the spot.

Suddenly the door was thrown open as the Countess of Crenshaw walked in, the door banging the wall as it flew back. Mena and Garrett turned to look, eyes wide with surprise. They had been discovered in the full throes of passion.

There was no denying it. They had been caught. They would be forced to declare an engagement, or Mena would be entirely ruined in society and Garrett...would honestly be completely untouched. The injustice of that left a bitter taste in her mouth.

The countess released a squawk loud enough to alert more people. Mena sprung back from Garrett and hurried to set her clothing to rights. It wasn't much use, as it was obvious what had been going on. Garrett looked fine, of course, appearing much as he usually did except for a slight color cresting his cheekbones.

Lady Claire came in, followed closely by Mena's father. Thankfully no one else followed. Perhaps Mena wouldn't have to die of embarrassment just yet.

"Well. This is awkward," she commented dryly.

Her father shot her a dark look, willing her to be silent. Mena looked away, tamping down her growing anger. Her father had made her a promise long ago that he wouldn't force her into marriage. She had come here to support him, but she would not be pushed toward the duke, no matter how badly her reputation might fare.

Sir Harvey-Morton cleared his throat and addressed Garrett. "I trust this will be handled appropriately."

It wasn't a question.

The duke shifted. She could see his hands bulging in his pockets, obviously pulled tight into fists. Mena observed him covertly while pretending to study the drapes. The window dressings alone cost more than her entire wardrobe. What madness had possessed her to dally with such a man? Lord, she had really stepped in it, and badly this time. Perhaps this was her worst error to date.

"Sir Harvey-Morton...I was hoping that we could all...pretend this never happened," the duke said quietly.

A heavy silence followed his words. Lady Claire stood calmly, a lady through and through, but her eyes flicked between the four people before her—Mena, Garrett, the Countess of Crenshaw, and Sir Harvey-Morton—as she twisted her fingers together.

Sir Harvey-Morton drew himself up, his jowled face turning scarlet as he worked himself into a righteous outrage. Mena needed to intervene. End this farce.

"Father," she said as firmly as she could. Four sets of eyes swiveled to her, and Mena tried not to squirm under their scrutiny. She cleared her throat and kept going. "I will not be forced into marriage. You promised me that I could make my own choice."

"And I have honored my promise, Mena. But this goes beyond the pale. You cannot weather the scandal alone. And mark me, scandal is unavoidable. I will have you protected."

"I don't need anyone's protection. I live my own life," Mena clipped.

Her father barked a humorless laugh.

"And tell me daughter, how do you plan to accomplish that? You have no money, no skills, nor experience. Would you live off the charity of your friends? Or simply live in squalor, to prove a point? Don't be stupid."

Mena's eyes grew wider with each word that fell upon her burning ears. Shame swamped her until she wished the floor would open up and swallow her whole. She bit the inside of her cheek, tasting blood, needing the pain to stop the tears that pressed at the back of her eyes.

"Your daughter is anything but stupid, Sir Harvey-Morton," the duke spoke, his voice hard. "If Mena chooses not to accept my hand, I will respect her decision as her own. But I am offering my hand, Mena."

Mena raised her eyes to his in surprise. The intensity of his gaze sent warm shivers down her spine. She was certainly attracted to him, and he said the right words. But could she trust him?

"Thank you, your grace," she managed, her throat constricted with emotion.

"You will not walk away from this so easily, your grace," Sir Harvey-Morton said. "My daughter is not some country trollop available for a bit of fun before you head back to London for the season. She is the daughter of a vicar, and a respected member of the community. I will not allow this slight against my family, sir."

"Regardless of what you might think, I am not a rogue. I do not ruin women for sport," the duke growled.

Drawn up to his full height, looking down his nose at her father, he was a picture of intimidating nobility, with a dark look in his eyes. Like an avenging angel about to hurl lighting down onto the earthly sinners below. Unfortunately, her father was far too stubborn to change course now. He would die on this hill, facing down his foe.

"Don't imagine that by offering your hand, you are proving your goodness. I expect you to follow through with doing what's right. There won't be any change of mind from you, when you no longer have this audience," he said, gesturing at the others gathered with a grim smile.

It was a clear threat to the duke's good standing in society, a promise to destroy his reputation if a wedding failed to ensue. Blessedly, Lady Claire stepped in, attempting to broker peace. She laid a delicate hand on her brother's arm, smiling sweetly between the two frowning men.

"Let us declare an engagement. That will stop any wagging tongues from spreading rumors of a scandal and will allow Mena some time to think on the proposal," she said, smiling with forced brightness, imploring all to agree with her plan.

Sir Harvey-Morton pursed his lips in thought and cast an assessing eye over the duke and his sister, searching for a trick. He was no fool.

"And what if I do not consent to the marriage?" Mena asked, inviting another scowl from her father.

Lady Claire's smile dipped slightly, but her eyes held a warmth that seemed genuine.

"If you choose to break the engagement, it won't ruin your reputation. Though people might wonder what insanity has taken hold of you, to shun such an advantageous marriage. But it won't harm Garrett at all; a duke can easily weather the gossip that would result."

The humor in her voice helped relax Mena, and endear her to the duke's sister immensely. She nodded in agreement, and hoped that her father would do the same.

"His grace will be marrying my daughter," he grumbled, but he uncrossed his arms with an air of defeat. "I will read the banns next Sunday. That gives you one week to decide, before it becomes public knowledge. Though I expect word to reach town before then. One week to woo your bride." He pinned the duke with a hard look. "Come to tea on Saturday." Again, it wasn't a request.

The duke inclined his head, but said nothing.

Mena wished she could faint, sparing herself from this humiliating circumstance. But alas, that was a skill she had never developed during her time at finishing school. Being discussed like an object to be sold from one man to another was hard on one's self-esteem. Mena tucked her feelings into a tight ball—the one skill she had learned at school—and stuffed that ball deep down inside until she felt in control again. No tears would be shed. That would be unbearable.

The sympathetic looks from Lady Claire didn't help much either. Surely the lovely Lady Claire would never suffer such embarrassment. Men must be lining up to beg for her hand, rather than her father forcing her onto unwilling suitors. Mena didn't want her pity. She needed her friends.

"Until then," the duke finally said. His eyes were on Mena.

She dipped into a perfect, practiced curtsy, and turned to leave without a word. Sweet relief to have escaped the situation flooded her senses as she walked swiftly down the hallway. Her father caught up with her and grabbed her gently by the arm.

"You could land a duke, girl. One with money, no less. Do you care about your future?" he demanded.

"My future is mine," she hissed, and pulled out from his grasp.

"Don't be naive," her father continued, though he kept his voice to a whisper, thank God. The last thing she needed was the other ladies overhearing this conversation. "I won't live forever, Mena. I am not trying to be cruel, or cause you unhappiness. But...I worry. You need money and protection, neither of which I can give you from beyond the grave. You want independence? Becoming a duchess will give you that in spades. And my feeling is that this duke would not displease you."

Mena flicked an irritated gaze at her father.

"I am going to my room to pack," she said.

Sir Harvey-Morton nodded.

"That is a good idea. I shall do the same, and we'll leave as discreetly as possible. We don't need to cause more of a scene than we already have. Just...don't throw this opportunity away so quickly. That's all I ask, Mena."

He appeared genuine, and Mena considered his words. It made sense. It was foolish to desire freedom. But she could muster no enthusiasm for this union. Her instinct was to run.

"We can talk about this once we're free of this place and I've had a moment to think. Do not press me," she said, and lifted her skirts to ascend the grand staircase.

"Fine," her father said, and he followed her up, taking his leave of her at the landing where the two main wings of the house diverged.

Mena was grateful not to encounter anyone else as she made her way along the hall to her door. Once inside she closed and locked the door, leaning back against it for strength as she buried her face in her hands. What had just happened? The agony of reality was starting to settle in. She was well and truly fucked.

Somehow, she would get out of this tangle. She would not be marrying the duke. Mena was determined to see this farce of an engagement over, and without a marriage.

She would be a terrible duchess. Mena wanted nothing to do with society and the drama of city life. She had seen enough at finishing school to know that it wasn't for her. She couldn't live life so stifled and watched by everyone. Besides, though the duke was a handsome—and skilled—man, he had no direction in life. He was lazy and privileged. Mena would grow to resent him, and Garrett didn't deserve that.

ena was angry mostly with herself. She knew better than to hope. Hoping led to expectations, and that was when she would most likely be let down. The sharp sting of disappointment nearly brought her to her knees with its force.

This was precisely the reason why she pursued self-isolation. She rarely disappointed herself, and even if she did, the sting was not so great. This feeling she was experiencing now cleaved her entire being in two, and she wasn't sure that she had the necessary strength required to get through this. What on earth was she going to do with herself now?

People often mistook her for a simpleton due to her quiet manner. The old saying rang true, however, for Mena's still waters ran very deep indeed. Men underestimated her. They thought that they could do as they pleased, and she wouldn't speak up. But they were very wrong on that score. Mena was not one to be crossed.

She took a steadying breath and willed herself to stand up straight. She touched a hand to her cheek and was surprised to find wetness there. The world was turning upside down. Mena never cried. Never. She shook her head, bemused, and turned to her writing desk.

She took a fresh piece of fine white paper from the stack and scrawled a short note to Clem. This missive was carefully folded, and Mena rang for a footman to take it and deliver it for her. Then she went to the wardrobe and threw open the mirrored doors. After pondering for a moment, Mena rang for a maid and finally learned to delegate.

"I am headed home within the hour," she said resolutely. "Please pack this up as quickly as possible."

The maid, Juliet, nodded, her eyes wide as saucers. To her credit she did not ask questions, and merely packed as quickly as she could. The clever girl had decided it was best to roll dresses and the like to cause the fewest wrinkles, and also save time. Something had happened, and a guest was leaving in a hurry, in the night no less, but Mena hoped she would have the decency not to make assumptions or spread gossip.

Mena chewed her lower lip, deep in thought.

Before the hour had even passed, Mena and her father were packed into the ducal carriage and clipping along down the drive. It wasn't until they had finally escaped the estate grounds that Mena allowed herself to relax. She would not change her mind now. They simply did not suit one another. She would not marry the duke.

Before long the carriage pulled up in front of the Harvey-Morton residence.

Mena turned the knob, opening her front door. The familiar smell of home hit her, instantly relaxing her. It was safe here.

A threadbare Persian carpet, faying along the edges, lined the narrow hall. No footmen or maids. Somewhere down the hall a clock chimed to declare the hour. The house was dark and still.

Mena bent down to pat her big hairy dog who had hefted himself onto aging limbs to waddle over to greet his humans from his bed by the empty fireplace. Mena scratched behind his ears, loving the downy fur of his floppy ears, murmuring praise for him but feeling…empty. Emotionless. As though she had spent her allotment of emotions and now was an empty vessel. How curious.

Just a few short weeks ago her beloved canine companion had been game to come on walks all over the village, and even to the orphanage, but time was quickly catching up to him and now he preferred to stay at home on his soft mat by the fire. Mena couldn't blame him, she often preferred to stay cozy at home as well, but alas was called out far too often.

Mena missed his companionship, but felt it was too soon to consider a replacement. That would be like telling her best friend he wasn't loved anymore, and she just couldn't do that. His loyalty deserved hers in return. She would just have to enjoy him at home, keeping her feet warm as she wrote her many endless letters.

Tonight was a time that she particularly was sad to not have his company, as she prepared to step out into the darkness of the night to seek out Clem's advice.

Sir Harvey-Morton came in then, shutting the door firmly behind him, causing the glass to rattle in the spider web style transom window above the door. He frowned down at the dog and began removing his overcoat.

"It is late, shall we retire to bed and discuss things in the morning?" he asked somewhat awkwardly.

Mena blinked at him.

"Alright," she allowed, having exactly zero desire to continue this discussion.

Her father nodded and looked up the stairs, though he continued to linger. Mena wanted him to leave, but she didn't want to cause suspicion, so she was forced to wait. Finally, her father sighed, and leaned forward to press a kiss to her forehead. It was an unusual gesture for a man so seldom accustomed to physical displays of affection. His gray mustache tickled Mena's skin.

"Good night, dear daughter," he said, sounding exhausted, and then up the stairs he went to his bed.

In a grand house there would be a servant to turn down the blankets and stoke fires before bedtime. But in this house, they were on their own. Mena took pride in doing for herself. She did not plan to go to bed just yet, but she needed to wait a bit longer before venturing out, so she headed to the kitchen to put on a pot of tea.

The kitchen was spotless, as usual, with everything carefully arranged and in order. Mena couldn't stand disorder, especially when it came time to do a job. The last thing someone wanted was heaps of dishes, pots, dirty dish cloths, and food scraps standing between them and a hot meal.

The neighbor had been in to feed the chickens and collect their eggs while Mena and her father were away, and it was late enough in the season that the garden didn't need tending daily, so Mena didn't expect a lot of work to do tomorrow there. But not having a cook had a huge downside: no lovely pastries waiting for midnight snacking. Or anything else for that matter. Not even a crust of bread in the house, disappointingly. She sighed.

The tea pot whistled, and she took it off the cast iron stove with a towel wrapped around her hand - practiced movements from a life lived at the edge of the middle class. She took a pinch of tea leaves from a worn metal canister and poured hot water over them. She waited for it to cool, staring blankly across the room as her mind whirred.

Upstairs her father had ceased his movements, his bed creaked as he settled in, and then a soft snoring filtered down through the cracks in the floorboards. Finally, it was time. Mena finished her tea and rinsed out her cup, leaving it on a towel to dry. Then she went to the front hall and gathered her cloak.

* * *

After Mena and her father had fled the house, and the countess mollified with assurances that Garrett and his new fiancé had merely been overcome with excitement following his impromptu proposal, Garrett finally withdrew to his study—a place he rarely frequented—to have a drink. Lord, he needed one after that scene. He grimaced as he forced a full glass of whiskey and sat in his desk chair. He drained half the glass in one swallow and set it down, bracing his elbows on the empty desktop, head in his hands.

Marriage. To a vicar's daughter. This was not how he had imagined this weekend playing out.

It was quite a way to thumb one's nose at the aristocracy. Marrying a country vicar's daughter of no reputation or accomplishment. Even her presence at the party had been an affront to the aristocracy. Garrett chuckled to himself as an idea occurred to him. He could elevate a commoner and force the ton to bow and scrape to her. It was too seductive an idea to not act on it.

Garrett had never thought he'd marry—he didn't want to participate in the ridiculous mating dance required of a duke. But now an opportunity had all but fallen into his lap, and he saw a way to avoid all of that nonsense. He could marry this woman, avoid the matchmaking mothers, the eager clasping daughters, and the boorish fathers of the ton.

And truthfully, Miss Mena Harvey-Morton was better than any other partner he could imagine—she was quiet, reserved, independent, and intelligent. She would be an excellent duchess, and was strong enough to withstand the meanness the aristocracy could dish out. Her flawless poker face indicated this, as well as what little he knew about her life.

Best of all was imagining the reaction of his mother. The dowager duchess had long been pushing for Garrett to select a bride, though one of excellent breeding. She was not a nurturing mother. She was indeed a bona fide creature of the ton. Claire bore the brunt of her meddling and controlling nature, but Garrett wasn't immune. And this was a way to deal with his mother once and for all.

Surely once he was saddled with a wife, she would give up attempting to steer him, and would return to her true passion—luxury and travel. And if the dowager did not return to travel straightaway, Garrett was confident in Mena's ability to handle his mother based on what he had seen of her so far. Mena had an iron backbone, despite her shy affect and quiet demeanor.

Claire would certainly be much happier to see their mother off on a trip abroad once again, so she could breathe. She didn't want to marry yet and was finding it difficult to spread her wings under her mother's watchful gaze. Garrett could help his sister in this arena by taking some of the attention off her to a wedding of his own, and so he would.

Of course, if Garrett married, he would also be letting go of his mistress. He was not the sort of man to carry on with another woman without his wife's knowledge, and he suspected Mena was not the sort of wife who would encourage that sort of behavior either. Garrett realized how little he had thought of his mistress since meeting Mena—which is to say, he hadn't thought of her at all. He was not sorry to be planning to break off their connection, as his thoughts were filled only with Mena and an absurd eagerness to spend more time with her.

Now he just had to convince his intended bride to accept him. Asking a titleless, rather impoverished woman to marry a young, handsome, wealthy duke wouldn't be too difficult of a persuasion, especially a nobody with nothing to recommend themselves.

A small part of his conscience reminded him that Mena was Thalia's friend, and Campbell might not look well upon his ill use of her. But no matter, Campbell of all people should see the value in marrying up. It was good for Mena after all, as she would have wealth and power beyond her wildest imaginings upon ascension to duchess status. She should be thanking him, really. And with that Garrett was resolved and put all his misgivings behind him.

Twelve

It was a short walk to Clementine's office, where her friend spent most of her time, even late into the night. Mena was not unaccustomed to walking the streets alone at night, but usually she had her dog. It was a bit unsettling stepping out into the darkness, but as the shadows enveloped her Mena found a certain freedom in the delicious shirking of social norms.

The streets were not empty, as there was always work to be done and entertainment to be had. Carriages rattled by on their way to bringing toffs to their various outings to rub elbows with the other toffs. A stray cat jumped from a second story window, startling Mena for a moment before her eyes adjusted to the dim light.

Beneath the glow of the streetlamps, men congregated, probably discussing which gambling establishment to visit next on their crawl through the village. Mena stepped lightly to avoid drawing their attention, and clutched her dark wool cloak tighter around herself, keeping to the shadows. The evening air held a crisp note, almost cold enough to require an extra woolen layer.

As she approached the building where Clem rented her office, Mena was relieved to see a lamp glow in the window, signaling her friend's presence. It was much preferable to visit Clem here rather than at her house where her father, Dr. Blakely, would also be present, as the man worked all hours and never seemed to stop for sleep. Mena didn't have any spare patience for fathers, or polite discussion, at the moment.

The door was locked, and Mena rapped lightly on the window. Clem was bent over her desk, furiously writing, long elegant brows furrowed in concentration. She jerked up at the sudden rattle of the glass, but relaxed her posture when she recognized her guest. She set aside her pencil and got to her feet. The bell above the door chimed as Clem moved to allow Mena to slip inside, before locking up once again.

"What a surprise," Clem said with a broad smile as she gestured for Mena to sit in the chair while she sat on the edge of the desk. "How was the duke's party?"

Mena sighed and plopped into the chair.

"That bad?" Clem asked, frowning.

The dark circles under her eyes gave her a ghostly look in the gaslight.

Mena considered how to begin.

"It was a complete debacle, to be honest. My father is demanding that I marry the duke."

Clem's jaw dropped open.

"What? How in the bloody hell did that come to pass?" she demanded.

Mena sighed, burying her face in her hands.

"It is ridiculous, and mostly the duke's fault. For some reason he has set his cap on me, and is attempting to take my hand in marriage," she grimaced.

"That is…interesting," Clem replied slowly.

Mena looked at her and had a sinking feeling that she would need to give details. She swallowed, her mouth dry.

"I was caught kissing the duke, and there were far too many people in the house to keep this quiet. So, if I don't marry the duke, I will be ruined and will be shunned by everyone in polite society."

Clem made a noise of surprise, and Mena cringed.

"And then he made an offer?" Clem asked sharply, ready to fight.

"Yes, he did. But…how can I marry a duke? I am wholly unsuitable," Mena blurted out with despondence.

Clem pulled her into a hug.

"You are absolutely worthy, far more so than any who wear the ivy coronet now. But if you don't want to marry this man, then don't. You can live with me, if it comes to that," she said, releasing Mena from her embrace but holding her gaze. "The duke is an idiot for not offering you marriage before he was caught compromising you, but that in no way reflects on you. You are a goddess."

Mena could have wept with relief that her friend would be a strong bulwark against this injustice, but she didn't want to prevail upon her friends. Perhaps no one would even remember that this happened in a few months' time, once another village scandal took hold of the wagging tongues.

"I thought you were of the opinion that marriage is unnecessary," she said, wiping a stray tear from the corner of her eye.

Clem waved that away.

"Yes, but he was looking for a wife, so if he wasn't honestly considering you for that role, why was he dallying with you?"

That brought Mena up short.

"Do you think he didn't consider me a candidate? But then why allow me to accompany my father at all?"

"Probably because he wanted to fill out the party with some people who wouldn't be stalking him in his own home. Most likely he invited your father for optics and gave no thought to whom else your father would bring along."

"So…what should I do now? My father is demanding the duke come for tea on Saturday and I am supposed to have an answer by then."

Mena looked at Clem. There was a familiar expression on her heart-shaped face; Clem was strategizing.

The feeling of relief she experienced knowing her friend was there to help was tempered by something else, some feeling she struggled to name. Was it disappointment? Was that possible?

"Alright, this is the best course of action," Clem began, "you do nothing, wait for the duke to come to you. When he inevitably does, because he's ever so gallant," Clem rolled her eyes at that, "You will tell your father that you will give the duke a chance, spend some time talking to him, before deciding. Then you will have satisfied your supposed duty to hear the man out and give you time to really think about this."

Mena groaned.

"That's it? I thought we were going to run away to South America together or something. My father caught us kissing—he's hardly going to believe that I'm not attracted to the man," she said before lowering her head to the hard surface of the desk. "Besides, how do you know the duke will turn up before Saturday?"

"It's instinct, I suppose."

Clem patted her back.

"I would take you anywhere you wanted to go, but I'm a bit stuck at the moment," she soothed.

"It's alright." Mena's voice was muffled by the table. She turned her cheek to rest on the cool wood. "It's a shit choice either way, really," she said softly.

Clem laughed at her language, but was nodding in agreement. "Which choice is less shit then?" she asked seriously.

Mena pulled herself back into an upright position and rubbed her eyes.

"I don't know yet," she admitted, nervous at the prospect of taking either road and regretting her choice.

* * *

In her bed that night, Mena lay awake struggling to parse her feelings for the duke and the prospect of marriage to him.

A hidden part of herself, a voice long suppressed, was whispering in excitement. Mena's heart rate increased, imagining sharing her life with a man so vibrant, someone who filled up a room with his presence. She would be connected to him in all ways, and they would know each other as intimately as anyone could be known.

That secret part of herself knew Mena didn't want to spend her days and nights alone for the rest of her life, even if her active mind insisted that she did not want to marry. In truth, she didn't want to marry for necessity. She wanted to marry for love, if she ever was to take such a serious vow. And at twenty-seven, she was fast becoming a spinster—a ridiculous concept—with her daily life not exactly lending itself to much interaction with handsome, eligible men. This could be her only chance at the life she'd always dreamed could be hers, despite her cynical rejection of the possibility.

But…Mena hardly knew the man. Yes, he was attractive, passionate, and gentlemanly, not to mention the obscene wealth and power that came with his title. All excellent reasons to throw herself at him like every other female, yet she held herself back. Fear of getting hurt stopped her. She needed him to prove himself a bit before committing herself legally to another person for eternity.

There. She was resolved to giving him a chance. That would certainly please her father. She closed her eyes to welcome sleep, but despite this resolution, her mind would not calm itself and sleep proved elusive. With a dramatic sigh, Mena threw off her blankets and set her feet down on the cold wood floor. Somehow her slippers always seemed to disappear.

She moved across the room to her desk where a stack of letters awaited her response. Mena pushed these aside, selected a new sheet of paper and began to write. Words flowed from her pen, soon filling the page and then a second.

When she was finished, Mena sanded them to dry the ink, and folded the pages into an envelope addressed to her old school friend. Unburdening herself was cathartic, and soon she was fighting back yawns. She returned to bed, finally ready to sleep, leaving the letter sitting on her desk for the morning post.

Thirteen

As he stood before his guests in the slanted morning light, giving them his good news, which was admittedly bloody awkward without Mena there to act the part of the happy bride-to-be, Garrett was struck by the reaction of his audience. The guests were utterly bewildered. They shot each other looks across the room, and some ladies even tittered behind their fans at the prospect.

"Her? A vicar's daughter?" a masculine voice asked no one in particular.

Sudden blinding rage filled him like an empty glass filling with water, rushing in to occupy the formerly empty space. Garrett pinned the insolent cad who was murmuring with a ducal glare, withering the man on the spot.

His gaze moved on, sweeping over the group, before landing on Lord Beckwith who stood leaning back against the far wall. The nonchalant slant of the other man's body, along with the smirk on his face, made Garrett's fingers clench into a fist. It was silly to let the other man get to him, but it was difficult when Garrett could imagine what Beckwith was thinking. Saddling himself with an unsuitable bride could only mean there was a very compelling reason to do so—and Garrett worried about how that reflected on Mena, who would no doubt bear the brunt of the rumors soon to come.

"Why on earth would a duke stoop so low when he could have any woman he desired?" a matron stage whispered with a malicious gleam in her eye.

Perhaps Mena was no stranger to such comments, but it broke something inside Garrett to imagine her being treated so poorly. He opened his mouth to speak when Claire came up to stand beside him, steadying him with a gentle touch. She lifted her chin, looking down her lovely nose at the assembled guests.

"I believe congratulations are in order for his grace. I am pleased with his choice. Miss Harvey-Morton is a pillar of this village, giving tirelessly of her time to local orphaned children, and her father is very respected. Let us have a toast in their honor," she said, prompting a footman to begin circling with a tray of champagne flutes.

"And where is the lady in question?" Lady Violetta asked with a knowing smirk.

Claire's jaw tightened in disapproval.

"Miss Harvey-Morton was needed at home, but we will be pleased to begin wedding planning soon," she said firmly.

The guests looked skeptical, but indulged their hosts in the toast, and began filing out to bed shortly thereafter. As they passed by the duke and his sister, they offered insincere felicitations on his upcoming marriage. A few of the ladies fluttered their lashes at him, and flashed tempting smiles as they headed out the door. Garrett smothered his revulsion. He refused to be the kind of husband who bedded every woman in sight without regard for his wife's feelings. He wasn't eager for matrimony, but neither would he callously disregard his vows. His guests' treatment of Mena also prompted him to want to be faithful in defense of her against this unfair treatment.

Once all the guests had filed out and were tucked into their carriages headed back to their own homes, Claire closed the door of the parlor and turned to Garrett with her brows furrowed in worry.

"That was interesting," she said, striving for a light tone, but her dark eyes were troubled.

Garrett nodded with a sigh and ran a hand through his hair.

"I didn't expect them to be so…"

"Judgmental?" Claire offered.

"Bloody hell, yes!" Garrett exclaimed.

Claire came closer and rested a hand on Garrett's arm.

"I love you, but you are woefully unaware of what life is like for the female half of the species. Miss Harvey-Morton has spent a lifetime being scrutinized and found wanting."

When Garrett opened his mouth to object to her assessment, Claire lifted a hand to silence him.

"I am not saying it is fair or valid, but it is the truth. She will have been plagued by the expectations of high society and appears to have been avoiding it for some time. It will not be an easy road for her, nor does she seem much interested in pursuing the ton's affections. Just know that what transpired in this parlor is but a taste of what is to come. So, get prepared for it, dear brother."

She reached up to cup his cheek, having to lift herself onto her tiptoes to do so. Garrett pulled her into a warm hug, because he suddenly felt the weight of his responsibility in a way he had not before, and because he needed comfort. It was a lot for one person to bear, despite the obvious privilege that came with it.

* * *

The afternoon sun was beginning its slow descent across the early autumn sky as Garrett knocked on the door of Campbell's new home in the village. The door opened revealing a crisply dressed maid in an expertly starched cap and apron.

"Good day, would you tell Mr. Marlowe and his lovely bride that the Duke of Bedford is here for a visit?" Garrett asked, flashing a winning smile.

"Oh, your grace," the woman exclaimed, hurrying into a deep curtsy which caused her to wobble on unsteady legs.

Her cheeks were stained pink as she waved Garrett inside. The front hall was painted stark white, which gave it an air of freshness, and a simple vase of autumn wildflowers sat on a long table by the wall. A staircase led upstairs. Garrett waited for the maid to lead the way. Her eyes flicked over him again, failing at her attempt to be covert.

"Follow me, if you please, your grace," she said, and began her ascent up the stairs to the first floor.

She led him to a door that revealed a lovely little sitting room painted a shade of teal that reminded Garrett of the seaside. Though the happy couple had only recently moved in, the parlor was decorated by an expert hand.

"If you would wait a moment, your grace, I will tell the master and mistress of your arrival."

The maid bobbed another curtsy and fled, leaving Garrett alone. He turned in a slow circle, taking in the cozy atmosphere. He struggled to put his finger on what felt so different about this place from his own residence.

Then it dawned on him. This was a home, for a family. There was love here.

That thought sent a spike of fear coursing through his veins, and Garrett looked toward the door, contemplating escape. He didn't know if he could face a couple in love just now. Even as he strategized to secure his own bride, he was still adverse to the institution.

Suddenly the door swung open, and in swept Thalia and Campbell. Garrett's chest squeezed uncomfortably as he assessed their general demeanor and was hit with the full force of their matrimonial joy. Thalia fairly glowed, her cheeks brushed daintily with pink. Her eyes kept sweeping over to meet Campbell's, their connection palpable, like an electrical current running between them. Garrett's jaw clenched. This was going to be awful. Campbell came over at once, and clapped Garrett on the back.

"Glad to see you here for a visit."

"Yes indeed. Welcome, your grace." Thalia smiled widely and sat on the settee with her pink and white lace cotton skirts deftly tucked in to leave room for her husband.

Garrett selected a comfortable looking high-backed chair and unbuttoned his jacket as he lowered himself. Campbell looked like his usual stone-faced self, but anyone who knew him well enough could see the happiness settled upon his broad shoulders, and the maddening twinkle in his eye. Marriage agreed with him, then.

"I could hardly wait for you two to return. It's boring around here without you," Garrett complained with friendly cheer.

"We weren't gone for long," Thalia laughed, and leaned forward to pour tea for her guest. "Hardly a week by the seaside."

The couple shared a conspiratorial look, ending with Thalia's cheeks blushing radiantly.

"Garret, are you sure you lacked company while we were away?" Campbell asked, the corners of his mouth playing at a smirk.

Garrett glared at his friend, longing to tackle him and deliver a few punches. Perhaps that would release this pent-up energy he was suffering from. He just needed a good fight. Was there a boxing club in town?

Thalia raised a brow and tilted her head slightly. Oh, bloody hell, now he was going to have to talk about it.

"What's my husband implying, your grace? Were you up to something?"

"Unfortunately, I had guests at the estate. A certain weekend party, if you recall."

"Yes, of course. I made hundreds of chocolates for it, if you'll recall," Thalia repeated his words back to him, even lowering her voice a notch to imitate his tone.

"Ah, right," Garrett stumbled, and rubbed the back of his neck. "Well, it was…interesting."

He sipped his tea and waited out the silence.

"That's all you're going to say?" Campbell finally demanded.

Garrett sighed and set down his cup.

"It was a bloody nightmare, Campbell!" he fairly shouted, causing Thalia to jump in surprise. "I invited all those women to the estate for you, and you left me alone with them." He forced himself to lower his voice and take a deep breath. "It did not end well."

Thalia looked at him with pity and offered him a plate of tarts as consolation. Garrett took one, but only because they looked so good. He took a bite, and was not surprised by the delicate flake of the crust and sweet tang of the fruit filling. He was almost grumpy about its perfection.

"What happened, your grace?" Thalia asked gently.

"I might have compromised someone. Accidentally, of course," he hurried to clarify.

"Bloody fucking hell, Garrett," Campbell breathed, and rested his head back on the settee.

"Quite," Garrett bit out through clenched teeth.

"Who was it?" Thalia asked. "Do you like her, at least?"

Always an optimist, Thalia looked hopeful as she blinked across the low table at him. Campbell remained as he was, braced for the news with his eyes closed. Garrett couldn't guess the coming reaction to his revelation, and the uncertainty made him incredibly anxious. He swallowed.

"Miss Harvey-Morton."

The name landed like a brick in the room, leaving the atmosphere tense, anticipating something.

"Mena?" Thalia asked, her voice oddly high, her blonde brows almost disappearing into her hairline in surprise.

"Yes," Garrett affirmed with a nod, struggling not to squirm with guilt.

"What the fuck have you done?" Campbell exploded, jumping out of his seat in a sudden burst of energy from his formerly still form.

Garrett lifted his hands, palms flat in beseechment.

"Let me explain!"

Campbell looked fit to beat him to death, but Garrett was fairly confident that his friend wouldn't do that. At least he sincerely hoped it was true. Thalia looked less angry than Garrett had imagined, which gave him yet more hope that this would be weathered swiftly. She grasped her husband's hand, and gently pulled him back down to sit beside her, and patted his leg. Garrett was fixated on that intimate view into his friend's marriage and struggled to gather his wits for defense.

He opened his mouth but couldn't seem to organize his thoughts in a coherent way.

"I don't know what happened…" he began, and opened his mouth to speak again but no sound came out.

"Do you enjoy her company?" Thalia asked.

"Yes, she is quite interesting and entertaining. We kissed…" Garrett spread his hands, "And were caught."

"But you did the right thing?" Campbell prompted.

"Of course!" Garrett exclaimed. "I agreed to marry her, but Miss Harvey-Morton is proving difficult."

Thalia snorted, and focused on refilling the tea cups.

"Garrett, don't be an ass. Mena isn't hysterical for not wanting a forced marriage to a man she doesn't know. Hell, she likely is the last person on the earth who would want to be a duchess."

"But why?"

Thalia speared him with a look.

"You've only just met, but you must know this about Mena, she is incredibly shy and avoids people as a rule. It would not have been an easy decision for her to even attend the party at all. She would have a natural disinclination toward living in high society."

Garrett sat with that for a moment.

"So, what should I do? I want her to be protected, and I do need a wife eventually. It seemed like a good situation for both of us, but I won't drag her to the altar."

Thalia shot him a quizzical look, one golden brow raised.

"You must woo her, your grace," she said with a laugh.

"Most people put in actual effort to gain a wife, Garrett. I know this must be difficult for you to believe, but women don't just fall out of the sky desperate to marry non-dukes," Campbell said, his low voice hinting at barely suppressed amusement.

Garrett scowled. Obviously, he knew that.

"How should I go about it?" he asked hopefully.

Thalia's face shifted to sympathetic, and Garrett leaned forward eagerly to hear her wisdom. But Campbell interrupted.

"She should know that you want to be near her, that you find her special, singular. Why are you here and not with her?"

Garrett blinked at him.

"Because I need your help." He turned to Thalia. "Help me, please. Your husband is an ass."

Campbell growled, but Thalia burst out laughing. She threw her head back and clutched her stomach as waves of laughter shook her. Campbell's lips thinned as he watched her, but he was slightly mollified.

"I do want to be near her, Campbell. But she is the only female in England who is dead set against marrying me specifically, so I am humbly begging for assistance here."

Campbell softened a bit, though still looking like a stone carving. Thalia had finally overcome her humor and was drying her eyes on a handkerchief.

"My apologies," she said with a grin. "That shouldn't have set me off like that, but…anyways, I agree with Cam. You should make an effort to spend time with her. Talk, listen, show her that you are paying attention and care."

Her shoulders lifted in a shrug. Campbell was nodding in agreement. But Garrett was less than satisfied. He knew that women liked to talk and wanted you to pay attention to every word, he had a sister after all, but surely more was required in this instance. He needed tangible advice for convincing this impossible woman to marry him. He took a sip of his tepid tea, wracking his brain for who else he could ask for advice.

"Thank you both, I will do my best to woo Miss Harvey-Morton," he said, forcing a smile.

His friends looked less than convinced, sitting across from him in their intimate marriage bubble. It felt a bit lonely on the other side of the tea tray.

***

After the duke took his leave, Thalia turned to her husband.

"Well, what do we make of that?"

Cam shook his head slowly, "I have no bloody idea."

Thalia bit her lower lip, worrying.

"I was hoping they would take a fancy to each other, because I know they could make a good match," she said. "But it might also end very badly. I've never seen Garrett so…befuddled."

"That's one word for it. It's good for him to be shaken up out of the rut he's been in," Cam said with a low chuckle.

"That might be true, but I don't know if Mena will even consider marrying a duke. She detests high society."

"So, he's wasting his time. Well, Garrett does a lot of that already, so what's the harm?" Cam shrugged, clearly ready to put it out of his mind.

Thalia sighed. She was going to need to speak with Mena, and Clem as well.

Fourteen

Mena and Clem considered the bouquet on the table before them. A riotous arrangement of flowers lay on the crinkled brown paper they had arrived wrapped in with a simple jute twine bow.

It was a lovely assortment of blooms, but Mena eyed them as though they were a deadly viper. Indeed, according to the language of flowers, there was deep meaning to be parsed here. She had rushed to Clem's office with the offering as soon as the liveried footman who delivered it had driven away in one of the duke's carriages, the elaborate crest on the side flashing cheerfully in the sunshine.

A simple white card had been included, reading: *You have witchcraft in your lips.* G. Clem, reading over Mena's shoulder, sighed in a most annoying way. Mena turned, scowling.

"I'd appreciate it if you weren't so inclined toward romance at the moment," she grumbled. "I need you to be impartial, not starry-eyed."

"Your duke is quite taken with you," Clem commented, her full ruby lips curled up in a devious smile.

Mena's frown deepened. She had other plans for her day before that footman dropped this ridiculous sentiment into her lap.

"He is not my duke," she corrected tartly.

"He clearly wants to be."

"What should I do? Can I simply ignore him and hope he goes away?" Mena asked glumly.

Clem patted her shoulder sympathetically.

"You should do whatever you wish to do, Mena. But perhaps you should actually take a moment to consider the idea of marrying this duke. He is young, gorgeous if the rumors are to be believed, and has enough wealth to not be reduced to scheming. Thalia approved of him as well."

"Yes, that is true," Mena replied absently, lost in the memory of kissing the gorgeous duke.

"Is he a good kisser?" Clem asked, as if she could read Mena's thoughts.

Startled, Mena threw down the card, and crossed her arms protectively.

"Obviously, or I wouldn't have lingered in his embrace long enough to get caught, now would I?" she grumbled.

"Do you suppose the duke picked these flowers out himself? It's an interesting selection," Clem commented.

Mena looked at the bouquet.

"Flowers have a language all their own. I suppose he would have had input, so his message was conveyed correctly."

Clem peered closely.

"Are those tree branches?" she asked.

Mena felt her heart squeeze as she recognized the leaves.

"Walnut," she murmured, warmth spreading in her chest.

"Why?"

"They symbolize intellect."

"Oh," Clem said softly, her eyes warming in appreciation. "What else is there? I'm hopeless at these feminine arts."

"Well, the hawthorn means hope, and the ivy is for...marriage," she replied.

Clem jabbed her gently with her elbow.

"And those red flowers?" she asked.

"Those are Austrian roses," Mena said, swallowing against the sudden thickness in her throat. "It implies that the recipient is lovely beyond compare."

She rolled her eyes, feeling uncomfortable with such sentiment. No man had ever paid such attention to her. No man had ever pursued her, nor wanted to. This was all so alien and new.

"Why are there those odd sprigs of herbs in there?" Clem asked with a laugh.

Mena tilted her head, reached out to pluck a few of the tender leaves, and rubbed them between her fingers. She held her fingers under her nose for the smell and was greeted by the fresh green aroma of dill.

"Dill?" she asked, confused.

"That's strange. Why would he include that? It was obviously intentional, as there are little sprigs all over."

"Goodness, Clem, don't you ever read the books you have on your own bookshelf? I'm sure I've noticed a copy of Flora's

Dictionary somewhere here before," she said as she thumbed across the titles until she found the one she was looking for.

She pulled out the heavy tome and turned the pages quickly until she found dill. Her eyes widened as she read. She snapped the book closed, her cheeks reddening.

"It symbolizes lust," she said with shock, meeting Clem's eyes.

Clem's perfect arched brows were raised.

"Oh my," was all she said.

"This is madness. Utter madness," Mena breathed.

"Do you want my honest opinion?" Clem asked.

Mena met her eyes and nodded. Clem took her hands and squeezed.

"You don't have to marry this man, or any other. You will always have a home with me if you should wish for it. But life is too short to forgo pleasure, and this man wants you. If you want him too, then go for it, my love."

Mena chewed her lower lip. Clem was serious. Could she do such a thing? Could she take pleasure and hold her head high? She wasn't confident and strong like Clem, and she didn't have a livelihood to occupy herself with either.

But if she were being truthful, she did want this duke. She longed for the feel of his hands on her, his lips and tongue giving her sweet torturous delight.

The bells chimed then as the door swung open, letting in both the commotion of the busy village street and Thalia. Clem cried out and ran to pull her friend into a tight hug, which Mena jumped up to join. It felt good to be together again.

"I am sorry to have neglected you both for so long!" Thalia exclaimed, her blue eyes brimming with tears of joy.

"Oh, don't be silly," Clem said sternly, "you were taking some time to enjoy your new position, and several other positions as well, I'm sure."

Thalia choked on a laugh and swatted her friend with her small beaded reticule.

"Cheek!" she said and turned to Mena with a smile. "And how was the duke's little party?"

Something in her expression told Mena that Thalia knew. Which was impossible, unless…

"He paid you a visit?" she asked with a groan.

Thalia chewed her lip.

"Yes, he came by for tea yesterday. For what it's worth, he clearly wants to marry you…and I don't believe it is duty that drives this desire."

Mena and Clem shared a look. Clem wore a triumphant smile.

"I knew it!" she exclaimed in satisfaction. "The man is smitten, and you are going to be the toast of London."

"Don't be silly," Mena breathed, feeling her chest squeeze with some difficult to decipher emotion. "Now, how is married life?" she asked Thalia, who laughed brightly.

"I am enjoying it immensely," Thalia answered with a happy smile.

"I miss our evenings together," Clem grumbled as she set about straightening the papers on her desk. "Everyone is off flirting with men and here I am all alone."

"Don't be dramatic," Thalia said with a laugh. "You'll find someone who will twist you up in knots and make your evenings fun again."

Clem started, turning wide eyes to her friends.

"Never," she declared.

Thalia shot Mena a knowing look, but dropped the matter.

"So Mena, what have you got there?" she asked, angling her head to see the bouquet.

***

Garrett sat at his enormous mahogany desk glaring at the pile of correspondence he was obliged to reply to. As a younger man, he had assumed that the moniker "gentleman of leisure" implied less work and was surprised to learn that there were actual expectations of him as a duke. This was the entire reason why he had hired Campbell in the first place, and now the man was leaving him in the lurch.

Garrett rubbed a hand through his hair, causing the curls to fall haphazardly over his scowling face. Was it too early to start drinking? God he was bloody lonely. Perhaps he should return to London and forget about all of this. His mistress would no doubt welcome him back with open arms.

But no, he did in fact have a conscience, and wouldn't leave the many people who apparently depended on him. And somehow, he already knew that any other woman wouldn't be able to distract him from thoughts of Mena. She was all he really wanted. A knock at the door interrupted his train of thought.

"Yes?"

The door opened and the head footman, Simon, entered, along with Bart, the boy from the orphanage that Cam had brought on to impress Thalia. Garrett had come to really enjoy having the boy around. In his hands, the boy carried a small vase of flowers. Except it wasn't a vase, but a pitcher, Garrett realized when it was placed on the desk before him.

"Thank you, both. Who sent these?"

"Young Bart brought them along with him when he arrived, and insisted on delivering them himself, per his instructions from the sender," Simon replied with a quick bow.

Garrett sat back in his chair and considered the jaunty yellow bouquet. Yellow for friendship. He hunted for a card, and finally found it stuffed into the blooms. It was a torn off scrap of paper.

I shall not lead you on, your grace. Please take this as a genuine sentiment. Mena.

Garrett frowned and tossed the scrap of paper onto the desk. Simon waited a moment, and then made a silent escape. Garrett crossed his arms over his chest. So, Mena was intent on keeping him at arm's length. Flowers implying friendship, sent from the orphanage rather than her home.

He sat there, considering his next move. Though why he couldn't let her go, he wasn't sure. He told himself it was about being honorable and responsible. But that wasn't really the reason.

* * *

Mena opened her front door and almost kicked over a small jar of flowers sitting on the top step. She glanced around quickly but saw no one who might have left it. Bending down to pick it up, she saw the card attached to the string around the wide mouth of the jar, and instantly recognized the handwriting. It simply read "G." Mena raised a brow, seeing the telltale blooms of a courting bouquet: tiny pink roses, cornflowers, and Sweet William.

She was tempted to dump the arrangement out onto the street, but stopped herself and instead went back inside the house to place it on the hall table. The man was incorrigible. Now she needed the walk to the orphanage to clear her head and decide on her next course of action.

A smile curved her lips as she found the perfect response. She almost laughed out loud, wishing she could be a fly on the wall to witness the duke's reaction.

Chapter

Fifteen

Garrett strode up the gravel drive to the estate house, removing his riding gloves as he went. He could feel sweat sticking his shirt to his back, and he was eager for a hot bath. As he approached the door, long legs taking two steps at a time, the door swung open by the butler, Moseley.

"Ah, your grace. A package arrived for you while you were out," he said in his typical flat tone.

"Thank you, Moseley," Garrett said as he entered.

The package was slim and wrapped in brown paper and jute twine. It weighed almost nothing. Garrett tore into it and discovered a small handful of pale purple wildflowers.

"Mosely, what is this?" he asked, sniffing the blooms.

The butler took a close look, bushy eyebrows drawn together. It was a wonder the man could see at all through that wilderness of hair.

"It appears to be yarrow, your grace."

"Who sent it?"

"It came with the butcher about an hour ago when he came with the weekly delivery."

"Thank you, Moseley," Garrett said, confused, and he continued on his way to his rooms, holding the yarrow gingerly in one hand.

He strode up the staircase and along the hall, his long legs making short work of the distance. As soon as he entered the ducal suite, Garrett tossed the gloves onto a chair and peeled his jacket off. He sat on the edge of his massive bed and began removing his boots. Harris, his valet, entered a moment later. He began picking up after Garrett, setting the room to rights again.

"Harris, what does yarrow signify?"

"I believe it is intended to convey a broken heart," Harris replied as he rummaged through a chest of drawers for fresh linens. "It is renowned for its healing properties."

Garrett considered this as he finished removing his second boot and started in on his neckcloth.

"If a woman sends a man yarrow, might it imply that she is giving him a cure for his broken heart? Because Mena couldn't have meant that her heart is broken. She's the one resisting my charms," Garrett said, speaking mostly to himself.

"I would agree, your grace. The yarrow would signify a sort of apology for not accepting your advances," Harris said sadly.

Garrett rubbed a hand over his face. What was he to do? He was trying to make things right. He couldn't force the woman to marry him, and he should be glad that she was intent on refusing him. And yet, Garrett was not pleased at all. It wasn't merely his pride and vanity that was feeling the sting of her refusal, but something deeper. He realized that he wanted Mena to like him, because he *liked* her.

"Your grace, Mr. Marlow and his wife are coming to tea. Should I lay out the blue or the green coat for you?" Garrett's intrepid valet asked, interrupting the duke's depressing thoughts.

"I don't care," Garrett said.

He stood and walked to the adjoining bathroom door where he would be greeted with hot water on demand without the bother of asking servants to lug buckets up the stairs. Modern plumbing was surely the best invention of the century. Garrett threw off his clinging shirt, soaked with sweat, and stepped out of his trousers. Harris followed along behind, picking up the articles as they were tossed.

"I shall lay out the green for you, your grace. Is there anything else you require?"

"Ask the gardener for a few sprigs of hawthorn please. I'll need it sent over to the vicarage before dark. No note," Garrett replied.

"Not giving up hope yet, your grace," Harris commented with a slight smile.

Garrett turned and grinned at his valet.

"Never," he replied.

Garrett turned the ornate brass tap, letting loose a fierce flood of water. He waited a moment to ensure the temperature was rising before plugging the drain in the large porcelain tub. Once the bath was half filled with steaming water, he swung a leg over the side and lowered himself in with a hiss of satisfaction.

Garrett knew that he was a handsome man. He was the sort of man women of all ages and backgrounds fawned over. He caused a ripple of blushes through a crowd of women when he entered a room. He was also fun. He was lively and witty. Paired with his obscene wealth, it was hard to understand why some plain country chit was so dead set on avoiding marriage to him. He was practically throwing himself at her for God's sake, yet she resisted him at every turn. It was giving him a bit of a complex, to be honest.

Though, she didn't resist him at every turn, now, did she? She was the very opposite of resistant when she was in his arms kissing back as bold as a merry widow. Garrett was rocked by a wave of lust at the memory of Mena in his arms, all lush curves and soft breathy moans. He wanted to know what sounds she would make in bed, when he kissed her all over and slid between her warm thighs.

Why he wanted her, in particular, so badly, he wasn't sure. But she filled his dreams and most of his thoughts during waking hours, too.

Garrett groaned and slid beneath the surface of the water, enjoying the silence. Perhaps the answer to his problem was to seduce his intended bride. She was far too cerebral, but he sensed—and had tasted—the passion that simmered beneath her stoic exterior. If he could set her free, unlock the wanton lass behind the mask, then surely she would see why they would make a good match.

Most marriages were depressingly passionless, but theirs would be so different. Maybe it could be like Campbell's...but for that Garrett would need to not only woo his bride, but to open himself up too. He wasn't sure he could do that, but he was willing to try. Willing to bet it all on a chance at happiness.

✱✱✱

At the orphanage, the long wooden table was covered with heaps of carrots, beet root, and parsnips. Mena methodically chopped her way through the lot of them, preparing pies for the children's dinner. A second woman kneaded bread across the large kitchen, her face dripping with sweat from her exertions. An orphanage full of children ate a lot of bread.

Fresh butter had been delivered from the village dairy that morning, and apples were placed as centerpieces on the long tables the children would sit at to eat. This was the best time of year, when the harvest was being brought in and the storerooms were full to bursting.

The door leading out to the kitchen garden swung open. Mena didn't bother to look up, keeping her attention on her work. It was probably one of the other maids coming in with something from the garden. But the heavy footsteps heading toward her didn't sound like any of the maids.

A shiver of awareness slid down her spine, and Mena turned. It was Garrett, sauntering toward her as though it were perfectly normal for a duke to grace the orphanage with his aristocratic presence. He was carrying flowers. Mena frowned, and turned back to her chopping, keeping her head down as she ruthlessly chopped and sliced.

"What did those carrots do to offend you?" Garrett asked as he leaned against the table, perfectly relaxed.

Mena ignored him. The maid who was kneading bread was pretending not to listen, but Mena could feel her intrigue.

"I brought these for you."

The flowers were pushed toward her, blocking Mena's view of her knife. She blew out a frustrated huff and scowled at Garrett.

"Excuse me, I'm in the middle of something," she said evenly, holding her knife down with the tip pressed into the wood of the table.

Garrett's eyes swept over the various vegetables littering the table, then raised a questioning brow.

"Surely someone else can do this sort of thing?" he said, clearly confused.

Mena rolled her eyes.

"It is my job today, and I need to get on with it. Please remove yourself."

"I was hoping you would give me a moment of your time…" Garrett said, his tone less certain, almost endearing.

"Why are you here?" Mena asked, hands on her hips.

"Uh, to see you, of course."

Mena pressed her lips together.

"Well, you've seen me. Now please leave."

Garrett hesitated. He obviously hadn't been expecting this kind of response.

"Is there a better time to return?"

Mena stared at him.

"Come for a ride with me. I've brought my new phaeton."

Mena grimaced, knowing that she would not enjoy a ride. While she loved horses, she did not love the wild sensation of riding one. And carriages made it all the more worse.

"Could we go for a walk instead?" she asked.

Garrett studied her, but nodded.

Mena crossed to the other woman, and spoke to her in a low voice, promising to return shortly.

"Never you mind, miss. Gladys can finish up for ye. Enjoy your time with your gentleman friend," she grinned as she swept a lascivious look over Garrett.

Mena led Garrett out of the orphanage, through the garden, and down an alley between the orphanage and several buildings before ending up at the edge of a farm field dotted with fluffy white sheep. They continued along the fence until they reached the woods.

Mena knew a little path that wound around this farm, owned by the Clark family. It was a beautiful walk, and she came here at least once a week with her faithful dogs for company. Now she had a different sort of beast with her, and her senses tingled with anticipation.

The woods were lovely and quiet. Only the sounds of songbirds interrupted the silence. They walked side by side, neither speaking for a long time.

Mena stumbled over a tree root, and instinctively grabbed Garrett's hand for support as she released a delicate "Aagh!" Thankfully she stayed upright, but a fierce blush burned her cheeks. Garrett did not let go of her hand, but kept hold of it in his own warm one. Mena found her attention focused singularly upon the texture of his skin—the strength in his fingers. Her mind began to wander, imagining the feel of them on other parts of her body.

She was going to need to dig deeper to strengthen her resolve.

Sixteen

"May I ask why you are so adamant about refusing my suit?" Garrett asked bluntly.

As a duke, he wasn't used to being refused.

Mena's eyes widened, and she looked down to where their hands were still joined, then gently pulled away. She cleared her throat and turned her gaze to the distance.

"When I was younger, I attended a very prestigious finishing school. It was my mother's fondest wish for me to be perfect in every way, and eventually win the hand of a very wealthy and powerful gentleman. This pursuit made me feel like I had little value beyond how I look." She paused to take a deep, calming breath. "I would starve myself all day, mostly subsisting on tea. But often in the evenings I would slip down to the kitchen, when I knew no one would be awake…and I would eat a lot of food. I would make myself sick eating. I was consumed with guilt and feelings of not being good or strong."

"That sounds awful."

Garrett understood very well the pressures of growing up with parents who had expectations. As the heir to a dukedom, he had been under immense scrutiny as a child to ensure he knew how to present himself as a man of power and wealth. His father had been especially difficult to please, leading to a fraught relationship.

"It was certainly a very dark time indeed."

Garrett found himself studying her profile, the way the sunlight cast shadows caused her creamy skin to glow. She was so poised, so self-contained, or at least she appeared that way. He had begun to peel back the veil, revealing what she so carefully kept hidden, like a dragon guarding its golden treasure. He wanted to know her.

"So, what changed?" he asked.

"My mother died," she said simply, lifting one shoulder with indifference. "And for a long time, my father didn't seem to care what I did with my life. It has been extremely refreshing…up until now."

She turned and leveled a frustrated look at Garrett. Her dark brown eyes were cavernous pools with no bottom. They were the eyes of a siren, luring men under false pretenses before dashing their egos on hidden craggy rocks.

"Fathers tend to draw the line at cads who ruin their daughter's reputation," he strove for a light tone, hoping to elicit a laugh.

"It is most annoying," she replied with a small curve of her lips.

Garrett's heart skipped a beat, and hope flared in his chest.

"My parents were not…the easiest either. My mother loves my sister and I, in her own way, but she was not a doting mother. I'm sure Claire would have a lot to say on the subject. My father…" Garrett paused to swallow down the bitterness that threatened to shake his composure; it was not something he ever discussed. "Well, he could be very demanding. As his heir I was under constant scrutiny once I left the nursery."

Mena studied him, her expression inscrutable, but Garrett sensed that she was listening attentively.

"There is much to dislike about society, lord knows I hate it at times. But there are certain freedoms that come along with a title. I'm sure you could put that to good use," he said, flashing a smile.

A ghost of a smile graced her lips as she nodded.

"That is an excellent point," she conceded. Then with a sigh, she said, "I am not against marrying you specifically, Garrett. I quite like you, actually."

An absurd bubble of pride welled up within him. Was he really so starved for her praise? Everywhere he went, people fell over themselves to show him deference and acclaim, and Garrett had grown used to it. Perhaps the desire for Mena's approval was because her good opinion meant more, and that she demanded more from him.

"The thought of having to attend events and even host…" she shook her head with a grimace. "It's very overwhelming."

"I don't do much of either," he replied earnestly, "You would be free to do as you wish, and a duchess is allowed to be a bit eccentric."

Mena opened her mouth to object, but Garrett rushed to say, "I mean, if that is your wish. I'm not implying that you are odd."

"I know I am odd," Mena said evenly.

Garrett was fairly certain she was being humorous, as there was a slight lift to the corner of her mouth.

* * *

They reached the edge of the Northern woods, where the train tracks disappeared into the thick foliage. Crickets chirped away in the tall meadow grass to either side of their little path. Up ahead a large oak tree loomed, standing in a solitary vigil. Mena led the way to the oak, and once she reached it, trailed her fingers over the rough bark.

"I used to climb this tree as a child," she said thoughtfully, tilting her head to look up into the verdant branches as though lost in memory.

Garrett cleared his throat awkwardly.

"I don't wish to pressure you in any way, but we should discuss something rather important regarding this marriage."

"I assume you are referring to consummation," Mena replied, and almost laughed at Garrett's expression. He was alarmed, perhaps by her forthrightness. "Spare me your shock, your grace. I am almost thirty years old, and I am not ignorant of sexual congress."

Garrett's eyebrows shot even higher, almost disappearing into his hairline, and Mena did have to laugh out loud. There was something both absurd and offensive about his reaction.

"I cannot help that I am shocked. It's certainly not a feeling I am accustomed to," he admitted, shoving his hands in his pockets as he spoke. Then tentatively he added, "May I ask how you have come to this knowledge?"

He was pointedly averting his gaze. Instead, he focused on the ground, as though it required his constant vigilance to maintain the safety of travelers.

Mena sighed, chafing a bit at the fact that she even had to say what she was about to. That it mattered somehow.

"You may rest assured that I am a virgin, but I have not lived my life in a convent. You might also remember that I have a married friend," she pointed out.

Mena caught the slight smile that Garrett was trying to conceal. She didn't know why it should matter to her how he felt regarding her innocence, but she experienced a surge of heat in her belly. He liked that she had never had a man before. Perhaps that meant that he wanted her for himself. The idea was a bit thrilling, to be honest.

"It's not something that I place value on, but I think it's important that we start out with honesty," he said.

Garrett stopped walking and turned to her. His mouth opened and closed a few times, like a fish gasping for air, as he rocked back on his heels and struggled to find the right words.

"Look, I know this isn't a love match, and we could very well wind up living separately. The best we probably can hope for is to be friends," he said in a rush before taking a deep breath and looked up to hold her gaze.

His face was so open and raw. Mena could feel her heart swelling, wanting to take him in and care for him like a lost puppy. Another one. She had rather a habit of taking in broken creatures, filling the house with them until her father finally evicted them in a most dramatic fashion.

"We shall need to make certain that this marriage cannot be annulled, and I hope that perhaps someday we might have a child, or two," Garrett finished, his hands still balled in his pockets.

"I have had similar thoughts," Mena responded, feeling a bit unsettled at this raw honesty between them. She paused, chewing her bottom lip. "I would very much like to have children. And given the circumstances that led to this mess, I'd say we would do well in that department."

Garrett's eyes heated at her words, and he subtly shifted his body into a predatory stance. Mena's pulsed quickened until her heart was hammering in her throat. Awareness pricked her skin and caused a shiver to run down her spine, igniting her desire.

"I am attracted to you," he replied carefully. "And I hope you feel similarly."

Mena could only nod in reply; she watched this man with wonder as he reached for her. She trembled with desire, needing his touch, her eyes fluttering shut as his arms encircled her, pulling her close.

And then they were kissing, Garrett's large hands framing her face as he took her lips. Mena gasped, pressing into his iron strength, and opened herself for him to explore. This kiss was more primal, more of a claiming than an exploration, and different than any other they had previously shared.

Garrett's fingers cradled her jaw with a gentleness that belied the raw need surging through him, evident by the slight tremor of his hands and the hard length pressing into Mena's belly. She moaned as she shamelessly tilted her hips against that hardness, reveling in the sensations exploding through her.

Together they sank down to the soft moss at the foot of a great oak, shielded from view of the path by its size. Mena stared up into the broad green leaves, which were touched by yellow at the edges now, as Garrett kissed along her throat and into her cleavage.

He pulled back, holding her gaze, bracing his weight over her on his elbows. This felt so right, natural, even. Mena reached up to pull his head down and kissed him as passionately as she could, pouring herself into the act, using her body when words failed her.

Garrett's hands were everywhere, roaming her curves, discovering her. Mena felt her skirts lifting, and eagerly moved to help him bare herself to his continued explorations. He skimmed up her legs, pausing at the top of her simple wool garters as though waiting for her consent. She reached down to take his hand and pull it to where she needed his touch, pressing his rough fingers to her molten core. His breath hissed through his teeth at the contact, his thumb brushed over the little peak of her desire with the barest touch. Mena growled in frustration, which elicited a laugh from her lover.

"Easy, love," he whispered hotly against her neck as his lips suckled her flesh.

His fingers expertly teased and caressed, claiming her as she writhed beneath him on the grass. She would surely have stains all over from this, but she couldn't bring herself to care, lost in the heady pleasure. Those clever fingers drove her senseless, bringing her to the edge of passion so quickly it astonished Mena, who was not ignorant of the ways of self-pleasure.

She bit back a scream as she came apart, Garrett's firm hands holding her to him as he rode out her pleasure, wringing every drop from her body until she lay limp, utterly spent.

Garrett grinned boyishly as he pushed himself up to sit, watching her with obvious male satisfaction. Mena sat up and shook her skirts out, letting them fall back over her legs. Her knees wobbled a bit, but she felt steady enough to stand, despite that earth shattering orgasm. It would have been normal to feel a bit awkward after that encounter, but Mena found herself feeling something else—she felt radiant and proud. Garrett had given her a kind of freedom she hadn't expected.

Mena struggled to find the right words for the moment, but needed to do something about the triumphant expression on Garrett's face. He clearly thought he'd won her over. But he hadn't, not really. Physical attraction and compatibility couldn't overcome the wide gulf between their lives.

"Garrett, I enjoy...what we do together...but you must know that we're not compatible," she finally said, striving for a gentle yet firm tone.

He shot her a look of surprise that turned to frustration, but he quickly smoothed his expression into the casually upbeat mask he usually wore.

"Well, I had hoped to be winning you over with my exertions, but I understand your point," he said easily.

Mena frowned.

"I mean it. We have nothing in common. What would I do as your wife? I would feel trapped."

She held Garrett's eyes, willing him to hear her and understand. This temporary connection they shared would not last. Surely he knew that. He should be off in London enjoying the company of opera singers and courtesans, not out here in the country wooing a plain, shy woman who had no interest in that world.

Unbidden, an image came to mind of hosting suffragette meetings in her London home. She could fundraise and coordinate. But that would mean changing her life so spectacularly...she just couldn't see herself doing it, taking that leap. She was frightened.

What she had told Garrett about her passions in life didn't even scratch the surface of her efforts. Mena secretly helped unwed mothers, prostitutes, wives escaping marriage, and others who needed aid by connecting them with the proper resources and benefactors. Her work with the orphanage was connected; it was, in fact, how she had come to work there to begin with.

Mena didn't trust anyone with this information, not even her closest friends. She didn't think Garrett would be an ally. Legally he would own her as property if they married; a nauseating thought. She could not betray the others, the women suffragettes and their cause. Garrett could jeopardize everything.

But then again, being a duchess would be powerful. Think of what she could do to help others, the money she would have at her disposal. It was a dizzying idea.

Her life here consisted of writing letters and attending meetings. Did she have it in her to hold charity events, fundraise, and stand up publicly? That was rather a lot, and it caused her anxiety to even contemplate it.

But surely that's what it would mean to be someone of power. She must use her privilege for good. It was cowardice not to seize this opportunity. Garrett was handsome, kind, passionate, and rather uncomplicated. Marriage to him wouldn't be a trial, and perhaps they could grow to respect and trust each other.

Was she willing to take such an enormous risk?

* * *

"Every time we are together, we seem to get into trouble," he said, pulling Mena up to stand.

She blushed deeper, and he couldn't suppress a grin in response. Whatever it was between them, lust was definitely part of it, and marriages had been built on far less. Perhaps being married to Mena would be more enjoyable than he'd already intuited.

"My father is expecting you for tea tomorrow," she said, looking away.

"Yes, I remember. Do you have any advice for winning him over?"

Mena looked at him then, a wry smile gracing her lips.

"Be wealthy and powerful," she replied with a shrug.

A peel of laughter shook his shoulders. Yes, it was rather simple sometimes.

"Alright, my lady. Shall I walk you back to the orphanage?"

She considered him for a moment, her eyes tracing over his face. He could feel the weight of those eyes. His breath held, waiting for her judgment. Finally, she nodded.

"You may, your grace," she allowed, and stepped closer to slip her hand in to take his arm.

They walked along in companionable silence, enjoying the afternoon light and the smell of wildflowers in the fields beyond the rough fencing to their left. Soon the gothic spires of village buildings came into view, then the shorter Tudor style buildings and the bustle of activity. The noise and smells burst their idyll, and before long it was time to let Mena go.

As they reached the orphanage's garden gate, Garrett bent over her hand, and pressed a kiss to the back just to enjoy the brush of bright pink that stained her cheeks. He wanted to tease blushes from her for days, but knew it was wiser to let her go for now. Mena tilted her head as she gave him a final look, then disappeared into the orphanage grounds, leaving Garrett to close the gate behind her.

Garrett watched her walk off, until she was lost to the lush greenery of the garden. He felt like a schoolboy again, with an all-consuming flirtation keeping him from his responsibilities. He growled in frustration, knowing the rest of his day was going to be filled with ledgers and numbers, rather than teasing and kissing.

Tomorrow, he would see her again. Tomorrow he would come to claim her.

Seventeen

The next day, they sat in the vicarage's shabby parlor. Mena poured tea, giving her father milk and sugar. She hesitated over the duke's, glancing over at him for guidance. He shook his head slightly and reached out to take the cup. Plain, unadorned.

Their fingers brushed, sending an electric currency through her. Goosebumps raised as the frisson of awareness washed over her skin. An image of Garrett crouched between her legs flashed in her mind, and Mena snatched her hand back, swallowing hard. Her hands shook as she poured herself a cup, causing a rivulet of hot tea to run over the edge, to puddle in the saucer.

For God's sake, she was having tea with her father in the room.

Sucking in a deep breath, Mena strove to gain composure. She kept her gaze from the man sharing the small upholstered sofa with her, sitting close enough for their hips to press together. Lifting her cup to take a sip, she was careful not to spill the contents of the saucer on her lap.

"This is delicious, I must get the recipe from your cook so I can enjoy these at home," Garrett said, after taking a large bite of the apple tarts.

Mena was rather pleased. It was one of her favorites too. She had taken some caramel Thalia had made and drizzled it over the pies just after they were pulled from the oven. It was heaven indeed, and seasonally appropriate, which always pleased Mena.

Unfortunately, she couldn't enjoy the moment, for her father decided to air their private laundry just then.

"Oh, Philomena makes those. She does all of the cooking in our home," he declared proudly, throwing her a confident wink.

Mena wanted to sink into the floor, her cheeks heating in embarrassment. Dukes didn't associate with people who cooked for themselves. It was bad enough to host a man of such wealth in these shabby surroundings, but to call attention to it by pointing out the lack of servants—it was too much for Mena to bear.

What was her father thinking? Did he want her to land a duke or not? Of course, she did not want to marry a duke, so really, she should just let him sabotage the whole situation.

"Is that true?" the duke asked, turning a surprised expression to her.

Mena chewed the inside of her cheek.

"Yes, it is," she replied flatly.

"I am incredibly impressed, Miss Harvey-Morton. It is very admirable that you possess such skills."

His easy smile warmed her, melting her insides like butter in the sun. She wanted to kiss him. What was wrong with her? She needed to get a grip on herself.

"Thank you, your grace. You are very kind."

Her father slapped his knees. "Well then, let us get right to the point. You will marry my daughter, as soon as possible."

The duke's brows raised in surprise at her father's bluntness, but Mena suspected he appreciated the clarity.

"As I made clear before, Sir Harvey-Morton, I will marry your daughter if she will have me," the duke said firmly, and turned to take Mena's hand.

She pulled away and avoided looking at him.

"We have nothing in common, your grace," she blurted. "I'm not at all convinced this is a good idea."

"Philomena, you must marry the duke. It is not only for your reputation, which I am aware you care nothing for, but it will keep and protect you into the future. I grow older every day, dear daughter. What will happen to you when I am a bumbling old man?" her father said, genuine concern shining in his eyes.

Mena huffed out a frustrated breath. "I am not incapable, father. Thank you very much."

"Sir, would you allow me a moment to speak with your daughter alone?"

Her father flicked a glance over both of them, but acquiesced.

"I'll come back in twenty minutes, and I expect you to behave," he ground out, pinning Garrett with a glare.

Mena almost laughed at the absurdity of the situation.

***

Garrett's heart beat wildly in his chest, adrenaline coursing through his veins. Really, he needn't be so nervous about proposing to a woman he had already proposed to. She wanted to refuse him, but he could see that a part of her was curious about accepting. There was no denying the passion that existed when they came together. She felt that too, he knew she did. But was it enough to sway her?

She sat on the settee, arms tightly wrapped around herself, eyes darting around, avoiding contact with his. He was charmed by her, drawn to her somehow. She would suit his purpose regardless, and he wanted her. There didn't need to be much thought beyond that. He just wanted her.

"Mena, I will not force you, and I won't beg," he began, taking her hands in his. Her eyes snapped up to meet his. "But I do want to tell you why I think we would suit."

Her eyes narrowed skeptically, but she was listening.

"I was not interested in marriage, but now that circumstances have contrived to bring us together, I find that I want to marry you. I admire your commitment to yourself, your honesty, your selflessness. We would suit very well, and I know we could be happy together," he said, speaking honestly though perhaps enhancing it a bit. "I would not ask anything of you that you do not want, Mena. As my wife you would be free to do what you please and would have whatever funds you require. I don't seek to control you, just to have the chance to admire you up close."

He flashed his most charming smile, the one that reliably melted all ladies in the vicinity. It didn't seem to have much effect on Mena however, beyond a quick glance and slight widening of her large eyes.

"What moves you, your grace?" Mena's voice was whisper soft, her eyes fixed on the tea service still occupying the low table before them, though the food was largely reduced to crumbs thanks to Garrett's enthusiastic eating.

"Moves me?" Garrett asked, baffled.

"Yes. Those big swells of emotion." Her wide eyes turned to meet his. "The crests of those waves, when your heart feels as though it may burst, and you have the urge to cry." She waited expectantly.

Garrett stared at her. How had he not noticed the beauty mark that sat just by the corner of her mouth? There was another one just by her ear. Mena was a curious woman, one whom you could so easily overlook and miss her hidden depths. Garrett was suddenly seized with gratitude that he was able to truly see her.

Mine, whispered a voice in his head.

"I'm not sure, Mena. I have yet to figure that out, but perhaps you could help me. Please give this a chance. I promise not to curtail your independence, and if you ever want to leave, I will finance that too."

Mena sat rigidly in her coffee and cream-colored dress; the velvety cloth practically begged to be caressed. And her dress was certainly caressing her lush body and covering far too much of her. Even her graceful throat was protected by the thick cloth. Before he could form the thought, Garrett lifted her hand, pressing a kiss to the soft skin of her wrist, where her pulse raced wildly, and inhaled her warm, clean scent. He murmured his approval, and heard Mena utter a soft gasp in response. That sound sent a jolt straight down to his cock, which responded eagerly.

Mena shivered. She acted so stoic, so tightly controlled, but she melted for him so easily. There was fire in her eyes. Her gaze dropped to his mouth, and Garrett gave what they both wanted. His mouth grazed hers delicately, barely touching at first. Then Mena growled, and turned fully into his embrace, pressing her lips firmly against his. Garrett slid one arm around her waist, locking her against him. The soft feel of her curves against his own hard flesh was so erotic, he almost lost control. He forced himself to let her take the lead, let her decide how this was to be done.

Mena shyly licked the seam of his lips, a timid demand for entrance. His lips parted on a sigh, holding back a groan at the first touch of her inexperienced tongue. She set the pace of their kiss, as Garrett held himself back, allowing the cautious exploration.

He could never have imagined the sheer excitement of being seduced by an innocent woman. She was just learning to follow her desires and seek her pleasure, and thanks to some god out there, she was experimenting on him. Garrett again thought of how lucky he was.

His tongue stroked hotly along hers, reveling in the sweet cinnamon taste of her mouth. Her breath fanned against his cheek as her fingers curled around the edges of his coat, holding him close as the kiss was transformed into one of bold, raw passion.

A creak of the floor in the hall alerted them to Sir Harvey-Morton's imminent return. Garrett forced himself to release Mena, and shifted away hoping he looked calmer than he felt. Mena straightened her skirts and pressed a hand to her cheek. She was taking deliberate deep slow breaths.

Her father loomed in the doorway, looking back and forth between them to determine the mood. He was suspicious, but nothing was apparent, so he sat back in his chair and studied his daughter.

"Well, daughter. What is your answer then?" he demanded.

Mena swallowed, dropping her hand down to twist with the other in her lap.

"I will marry the duke."

"Very good," Sir Harvey-Moton clapped his hands together in glee.

Garrett wondered how surprised the man was that Mena had chosen marriage. He looked at Mena, and she seemed to be thinking the same thing. Their eyes met, hers dancing with mischief. They shared conspiratorial smiles.

After tea Garrett returned to the estate. He had some important letters to write. One to his sister, to let Claire know everything was settled and she now had the pleasure of planning a wedding—albeit a swift one. He wasn't about to let this courtship go on and on and risk his bride getting cold feet. The second letter was to his mother, to bring her home from her travels. She would have his head if she missed the wedding. And finally, Garrett wrote to Campbell, requesting his aid as best man.

* * *

Mena went to Clem's office but found it dark and shuttered. She turned down the next street, heading for Thalia's. The tidy brick house was welcoming, with cheerful lamps glowing in the windows, and a crisply dressed butler opened the heavy door before her knuckles had barely made contact with the painted wood.

Thalia came out from the kitchen, wiping her hands on a dusty apron but beaming with joy. She enfolded Mena in a warm embrace.

"I agreed to marry the duke," Mena blurted out.

"And how do you feel about that decision, dear?" she murmured into Mena's hair.

Mena thought about that question. How did she feel? The first thing that popped into her head was cautious optimism—she was happy, but nervous. She took a steadying breath and stepped back, forcing herself to focus on the scent of vanilla that clung to Thalia from her baking, as she steadied her breathing enough to continue.

Thalia to release her.

"I feel happy, I really do. Though I can worry myself into a state, but I am hopeful."

Thalia studied her expression, but nodded.

"Well…that's good, I suppose. And I want you to know that you may not stay with him if you grow to be unhappy. I demand a promise right here and now, that you will come to me if you are ever anything other than joyful in your marriage."

Mena laughed, "So I can be forced to see you and Mr. Marlow in saccharine marital bliss constantly? I love you, and appreciate the gesture, but I can take care of myself."

Thalia twisted her hands together, clearly skeptical.

"Then promise me you'll go to Clem."

Mena smiled softly, and placed her hands on Thalia's shoulders, looking her square in the eye.

"I will. I promise. Now let's sit down and discuss something far more fun."

Thalia nodded, feigning excitement, but Mena could see the tightness of the skin around her mouth, and the tension in the set of her shoulders. But Thalia turned and led the way into the sitting room. It was a riot of pattern and color within, yet somehow sparsely furnished.

"The decor is not yet settled…clearly," she grimaced.

The women sat on the emerald damask settee that sat in the center of the room. It clashed almost audibly with the yellow and orange striped wallpaper and heavy red drapes. It made Mena's eyes hurt.

"Was this from the previous owner?" she asked, gesturing with her arm to indicate the room.

Thalia sighed. "Yes. The family who lived here before truly had a bizarre fashion sense. But I can assure you that I have samples for the walls and windows, and furniture already purchased and awaiting delivery."

"You are the one who must live with this assault to the senses, not me," Mena protested. "I rather like this settee, will you keep it?"

Thalia brushed a hand over the soft pile of the damask fabric, several shades of green swirling together in an elegant dance across the cushions.

"Yes, this settee is my favorite piece of furniture in the house. It needs to be shown off," she said, looking pleased.

Mena smiled back, feeling genuinely at ease for the first time in over a week. She let herself imagine selecting her own furnishings. It was small, but it would mean she had some control over her life, and surely that was something duchesses did. She could be content.

Eighteen

September was supposed to be a lucky month for a wedding. Somehow Lady Claire had produced one fit for a duke in three short weeks, with the chapel bursting with flowers and an enormous wedding breakfast planned, despite their incredibly short engagement. The pews were filled with people from the village, and as many friends and family as could come by train. Lush bouquets of late summer flowers burst from every corner and crevice.

Thalia and Clem had agreed to be bridesmaids, along with Lady Claire of course. They waited with Mena in the antechamber, shifting their feet nervously in their shimmering white dresses. Thalia clutched her bouquet like it was a lifeline in a storm, her eyes trained on the door that led to the aisle they would walk. Clem was fussing over Mena's veil, wanting her to be perfect for all the judging eyes and critical tongues that waited with glee to spread gossip to every corner of the country.

Garrett had Campbell and two distant cousins as his groomsmen. They waited at the front of the church in their morning coats and crisp white cravats, boots gleaming in the late morning sunshine that flowed through the windows.

The dowager duchess was in attendance as well, which made Mena positively nauseous with anticipation. They had not yet met, as Garrett's mother seemed to be permanently abroad traveling about and enjoying herself. But now the reckoning would come, and on her wedding day no less. Surely the older woman would take one look at Mena and turn up her nose, aghast at her son for his choice of bride.

Mena hadn't seen much of her fiancé in the past three weeks, either. He had presumably been assisting his sister in planning the wedding and preparing for Mena to join him in his home, but it had been disconcerting to have been effectively abandoned by him on the heels of a dizzying campaign to woo her hand.

Sir Harvey-Morton had been adamant that the banns be read for three weeks, as was traditional, but that the wedding would happen right after. Now here they were, about to join themselves legally and for all eternity. Mena's nerves made her feel like a thousand butterflies were trapped within her.

She had requested a simple white dress but was pleasantly surprised with what Lady Claire's seamstress had produced—an elegant gown with enormous puffed sleeves and a long train. Her hair was arranged in a fancy coiffure and adorned with a coronet of orange blossoms, then covered with a long veil, covering everything like glaze over a bundt cake. It felt ridiculous, and Mena's heart hammered in her chest, suffocated by the weight of this wedding.

What had she been thinking? She couldn't be a duchess! She had to get out of here immediately.

She turned to flee, her voluminous skirts clenched in both fists. But her father blocked the exit and there was no way to get by without having to shove him aside. Mena forced herself to take a breath and focus on something.

Her gaze landed on the sunbeam on the scuffed oak floor, turning the wood a lovely swirled honey color. Dust motes danced in the light, almost twinkling. Mena breathed and studied that spot on the floor until she could feel the panic subsiding, her limbs loosening. Then she was able to look up, straighten her spine, and prepare to walk down the aisle.

"Are you alright?" Clem whispered with concern, her voice sharp.

Mena took a shuddering breath.

"Yes, I'm perfectly fine," she lied.

Clem looked doubtful but didn't press. Mena's friends knew how much she hated crowds and attracting attention. This was going to be quite the ordeal. Mena pressed a hand to her stomach, willing the butterflies to calm down.

* * *

Garrett tugged at his cravat, feeling hot in the little village church with the sun streaming in to cook him right there in his boots. Was this what hell felt like? He caught the eye of his best man, who gave him a chiding look. Garrett left his cravat alone, and clasped his hands before him, determined to do his duty.

The pews before him were full of murmuring people and their eager, bird-like eyes. The papers would surely have something about this, a highly unusual event for high society. Most dukes had elaborate weddings at St. James's cathedral in London with all of the aristocracy in attendance, including royalty, and only after a month's long engagement—these affairs did take a long time to plan, after all—rumors were sure to be flying.

He wasn't certain what was keeping his bride, but after the young apprentice vicar cleared his throat in irritation for the third time, Garrett was growing a bit nervous that she wasn't coming. In the eyes of society, it would be a complete humiliation to be left waiting at the altar, especially by an untitled vicar's daughter.

He wasn't concerned with a few laughs at his expense. Garrett was solely focused on his deep and inexplicable desire to marry Mena. He wanted her to choose him too.

He and Campbell exchanged looks, but they stood where they were. Finally, there was some movement behind the doors that led out of the chapel as the ladies organized themselves in order, and the organist began to play.

Thalia led the procession followed by Clementine Blakely, the rather scandalous doctor's daughter who ran her small printing company. Each of them wore a white dress, high necked and plain, and held a righteous bouquet of white lilies, orange blossoms, and green ferns. As they passed by to take their positions each woman gave Garrett a look of intense scrutiny, not seeming satisfied as they turned.

Fucking hell, he thought.

The organist deftly changed the tune, announcing the presence of the bride. Everyone turned, almost in unison, and angled to see the duke's perfect bride. Mena stepped into the light on her father's arm and hesitated, taking in the crowd of people and their clawing interest. She visibly swallowed, and turned, lifting her chin to see Garrett. He felt the weight of her eyes when they connected with him, and he had to fight an impulse to go to her. But she had to do this on her own. He willed her to come to him, silently urging her along.

Mena took another tentative step, her spine stiff as steel. She continued her walk, looking entirely unemotional from the outside. Her father looked positively gleeful, preening under the attention as he marched his only child down the aisle.

Garrett knew she was finding this exceedingly difficult; her nerves were likely feeling quite chaotic. When she arrived at the altar, he felt his heart squeeze with joy, and he smiled down at her with pride. Mena looked up at him with a tremulous smile of her own, her eyes locked on his as though for safety. He was her line in the storm, and that made him feel absurdly protective.

Sir Harvey-Morton silently placed his daughter's hand in Garrett's, clapped him on the back, and took his position to begin the ceremony. The vicar cleared his throat and bade everyone welcome and please sit. Garrett took Mena's smaller hands in his; their icy coldness bothered him. He wrapped his warm fingers around hers, infusing her with his heat. Her pupils dilated, and her gaze dropped to his lips. Garrett was instantly aroused, and quite inconveniently so, in front of so many people.

He forced himself to look at his bride's father and listened to every word of his sermon on marriage and duty and patriotism. He wanted to elbow Mena and share a laugh about it, but tucked that away for later. This was already going so well, he congratulated himself—he and his wife got along and were attracted to each other. That was better than most society marriages, which were entirely about power and capital.

When it was time to speak their vows, Garrett felt a burst of some new emotion as he pledged himself to another person, and sealed the promise with a golden band he slid onto her finger. As she did the same, her quiet voice and delicate touch penetrated his heart, settling inside like a seed that promised to grow into something chaotic. A thread of fear coursed through him, but Garrett pushed that away, not allowing for one drop of uncertainty.

The ceremony ended with the call for a kiss, and Garrett's heart rate jumped up. He gently pulled Mena into his arms and tipped her head back for a thorough kiss. After three seconds she laughed and pulled away, forcing Garrett to release her, but he took her hand and settled it into his elbow.

They walked together back down the aisle, rather quickly as the crowd was getting loud and Garrett was eager for escape. Outside of the church a carriage awaited them, and a footman instantly jumping down to open the door. Once Mena was tucked inside, Garrett jumped in and tapped on the ceiling for the carriage to take off.

"Thank you for that swift exit," Mena said, her voice a bit breathless.

Her voluminous skirts and veil filled the carriage, and gave her the appearance of emerging from a pile of merengue. Her open smile was genuinely happy, and that pleased him immensely.

"That was for my own benefit as well as yours, but I will accept the gratitude just the same," he said as he inclined his head in mock solemnity.

"So, are we going to the estate?" she asked.

"Yes. My sister has arranged a wedding breakfast. It will inevitably last too long and we'll be forced to excuse ourselves before the guests finally leave. It's tradition. They all want to imagine us upstairs," he said, wiggling his eyebrows suggestively.

Mena gave him a look of disapproval, but he suspected it was to cover for her anxiety about the lengthy ordeal of dining with so many aristocrats. He doubted she had been pouring over Debrett's in her quest for a titled husband. None of that mattered to Mena. And that was one of her best qualities, her honesty and dedication to following her own rules.

"At least I know the food will be good," she said, with what sounded to Garrett like forced cheer. "What does the seating arrangement look like?"

"We will sit together, with Claire next to me and Campbell next to you. My mother will be at the head of the table, and your father at the other end. It won't be too awful, I promise."

Mena looked uncertain, but nodded. Soon enough the carriage pulled around in the estate's drive, and the footman opened the door. Garrett jumped out, and handed Mena out himself, keeping her hand once she was firmly on the ground. He escorted her up the steps to her new home and stopped at the door to scoop her up and carry her over the threshold.

Mena squealed in alarm, clinging to his neck, but her expression melted into dreaminess as he held her in his strong arms. Garrett pressed a gentle, tender kiss to her lips before setting her down again. Mena held onto him for a moment, staring up at him with a moonstruck look. Then she blinked and released him, stepping away. She looked around and caught sight of the butler and housekeeper waiting patiently.

"Oh, how embarrassing," Mena murmured, her cheeks heating.

Garrett took her hand again and pulled her over to greet the staff.

"This is Mosley and Mrs. Hobbs."

"Wonderful to meet you both," Mena managed through her mortification.

"Welcome home, your grace," Mosley bowed deeply.

Mrs. Hobbs smiled and curtsied, clearly eager to speak with her new duchess.

"We will be in the blue parlor awaiting our guests, excuse us," Garrett cut in before the women got to talking, and steered Mena down the hall.

The sound of arriving guests was already reaching them as Garrett settled his bride into a comfortable chair. He gritted his teeth. Now that he had her home with him, he was suddenly keen to be alone with her. Damn these ridiculous rituals he was forced to engage in.

* * *

The dowager duchess appeared in the door, looking as sour and unpleasant as she had during the ceremony. She walked with a gold-topped cane but was intimidating, nonetheless. Garrett went to her and kissed her cheek.

"It is good to see you, mother. I cannot wait to hear about your travels, but first come meet my wife, Philomena."

The dowager cast a critical eye over Mena, who dipped into an expert curtsy, keeping her expression carefully neutral. The dowager continued to scrutinize Mena for a moment before gracefully lowering herself into a chair, sitting at the edge of the seat, her elegant hands braced atop her cane.

"So, you are the new duchess," she clipped out.

"I am, your grace," Mena answered carefully.

"Well, you aren't much to look at," she stated, dropping the insult casually. "Are you accomplished?"

Mena could feel tension building in her neck, but she sat there and did her best to appear undaunted.

"As a graduate of the Henderson Finishing School in Kent I can play the piano moderately well and paint quite badly, and I also can sing abominably."

Garrett smothered a laugh but not before he coughed out a noise that caught his mother's attention. Her head snapped to the side, and she pinned him with a withering look before returning to her inquisition.

"For a school with an illustrious reputation they did a poor job by you, Philomena," she said, then paused to check the door for visitors before continuing. "The ton is not an easy place to exist within. You shall be expected to be flawless and without reproach. We will visit my modiste as soon as possible," she finished with a nod.

Mena was stunned. She had not expected…help. Mothers were for nitpicking, not providing direction or oversight, in her experience. Mena flicked her eyes over to gauge Garrett's reaction; he looked nervous, but trying not to show it. She turned her attention to the dowager.

"Thank you, your grace, for the insight. I look forward to our shopping trip," Mena replied.

The dowager considered her for a moment.

"You are not, in fact, as plain as you appear," she said finally.

"Mother!" Garrett roared, jumping up to stand. "You cannot speak to her that way."

"It was a compliment," the dowager protested, though she hardly looked concerned about her son's ire.

"It's fine," Mena said evenly.

Garrett looked at her, but she couldn't meet his eyes. It was ridiculous to still feel burning shame, even after all these years of being told she was plain.

"You are not plain, was my point," the dowager said in a huff. "You have a lovely chin and eyes. Your hair looks decent, though you should have it curled by your ladies' maid. And we must do something about all those freckles."

Mena opened her mouth to reply when the sound of several pairs of shoes in the hall came closer, and finally guests began appearing for the breakfast. They streamed into the room, and the conversation ended. Mena looked at the dowager, but the older woman had turned away to speak with someone else. Mena tried to think about her dog, walks in the woods, the smell of earth and rain, anything to keep her composure.

Nineteen

The wedding breakfast lasted for two hours before there was a glimmer of hope in sight. After Mena cut the cake, and several rounds of toasts, the women began to show signs of leaving the room. Once they took their leave it was a simple matter of ceremony for how everyone should take their leave. Mena went upstairs first, and Garrett counted out the longest ten minutes of his life before wishing everyone goodbye and following her.

He almost ran to the ducal suit, barely keeping himself under control. Once reaching the massive mahogany doors though, he hesitated before knocking and slowly opening the door. The room was empty.

Garrett walked completely into the room and shut the door behind him. The sitting room was designed as a meeting point to connect the duke and duchess's private bedrooms and dressing rooms. A third door led to the bathroom. He imagined leisurely baths together in the large soaker tub.

The next place to check for his wife was in her bedroom, but that too was empty except for the fire in the grate. He stalked to his room. The door was ajar, firelight leaking out. He pushed it open, slowly revealing his wife waiting for him on the bed.

She lay on her side atop the counterpane, striving for a seductive pose, but instead she revealed her charming innocence. Mena wore a long gossamer gown of white muslin that trailed down her body but hid nothing from view. Her shining brown hair was left unbound and hung down to coil over her trim waist. Her nervous state was palpable. Garrett closed the door behind him and locked it with a firm click. He approached his new bride as though she were a skittish fawn in the woods.

Garrett removed his jacket and boots, almost tripping over his feet in his haste. He rolled up his white shirt sleeves in practiced movements. Mena stared at his hands, her eyes wide. She swallowed, the movement drawing Garrett's attention to her bare throat, then lower to the curves of her full breasts tipped with berry-colored nipples barely concealed by her thin night rail.

He advanced, moving with panther-like grace, climbing onto the bed. She was his prey. He cupped her face between his large hands, tipping her head back to receive his kiss. As his lips melded with hers, Garrett almost incinerated from anticipation.

Mena's eyes fluttered closed, and she leaned into his strength. One of his hands stole down to hold her close against him, his fingers pressing into her lower back in a deliciously possessive way.

Their lips met over and over, growing in intensity with each breath, growing desperate with desire. Mena clung to Garrett like a vine clinging to a tall tree, plastering herself to him shamelessly.

What did it mean, that this woman drove him so wild? He was supposed to be in control, aloof, experienced. But now he was anything but calm, he was a creature of pure need. And Garrett was desperate to soothe the ache that plagued them both.

Mena whimpered, needing to get closer, to feel more.

Garrett's hands stroked over her hip, arse, thigh, reveling in the warm silk of her skin. He pulled the velvet ribbon that tied Mena's garters, slowly releasing her from the bondage of the day. She sighed as he stripped her silk stocking off, taking his time, drawing out the sensation.

"Tell me," Garrett demanded, his voice thick with desire.

"I want you," Mena said shyly.

Garrett looked down at her, pulse thundering in his chest.

"You want my cock?" he clarified with a growl.

Mena's eyes widened, her hands gliding over his biceps, the muscles bunching and flexing under her fingers. Garrett wanted to impress her, drive her wild. Her shy ministrations threatened to undo him.

"Yes, please. Garrett, I need it," she moaned, rocking against his thick thigh that was pressed between her legs.

Garrett shuddered with need, eyelids heavy as he looked down at her.

* * *

Mena was excited beyond belief at the effect her words had on the glorious man between her thighs. She felt powerful. Garrett leaned down and captured her lips in a searing kiss that ended with a moan as Mena clung to him, her fingers twisting into his soft curls. The kiss became fiercely possessive, and Garrett framed her face in his large, strong hands, taking her mouth in a crude imitation of what he planned to do with his cock, thrusting in and out with languid strokes that made Mena's toes curl.

Her fingers dug into his scalp, needing something to hold on to as the building pleasure threatened to incinerate her. Garrett slid one large hand down along her body, feeling her curves before sliding between their bodies. Mena felt the broad tip of his cock nudge her slick folds, rubbing along her pulsing seam. As he slowly filled her, stretching her intimate muscles in a new way, Mena held her breath. The intrusion stung, and she instinctively pushed against Garett's chest. He instantly stilled.

"Are you alright?" he asked, his voice strained, but his eyes held such tender concern that Mena relaxed back into trusting this man.

She smiled coyly.

"You're so big. I don't know if I can take—no!" she protested as he withdrew.

She wanted him, every piece of him, even if it hurt. But he wasn't stopping. Instead, he rolled over onto his back, pulling her with him, and settled her on his lap with her legs astride his powerful thighs. Mena felt so much more exposed this way, and she reflexively covered her breasts. Garrett soothed his hands over her body, easing her tension, and murmured his appreciation for her.

"You look so beautiful, love. Let me see all of you," he said, cupping her breasts in his hands.

He rolled the hardened nipples between his fingers, sending hot sparks of desire right to her core. Mena's head tilted back as she pressed into his hands, loving the sensation.

"Yes, that's it, love. Now come take my cock. Good girl," he crooned as he lifted her easily up onto his throbbing member. Her slick heat welcomed him, holding him so tight as she was filled by him. "I'm yours to use, Mena. Find your pleasure."

He showed her how to ride him, gripping her ass in his hands, spreading her so she could take him deep. Mena struggled to find a rhythm, but each stroke felt so blisteringly good, and

Garrett rose up to meet her, giving her what she needed. Mena forgot about embarrassment and worry, lost in the sensations and building pleasure.

She looked down at Garrett, holding his gaze as they fucked. Sweat rolled down her neck, and he moved up to lick it from her feverish skin. Mena gasped, grabbing his head to hold him there, and he gave her what she needed, kissing and licking along her throat and collarbone before capturing a nipple in his mouth with a stinging bite.

And that was enough to cause Mena to hurdle over the cliff in a spasm of pleasure so intense that she felt suspended in it. Wave after wave of glorious feeling rocked her, and she was reduced to clinging to Garrett for support. He growled in approval. Mena returned to her body, feeling limp, but her lover was not finished with her yet. He withdrew, and lay her down on the edge of the bed, her legs spread wide for him.

"Garrett, I can't," she protested weakly, but the sight of the muscled Adonis standing between her thighs caused the coil of desire to build again.

"Yes, you can, love. I'm not ready for this to end yet," he replied as he slid inside, stretching her sore muscles.

The pleasure was threaded with pain, and Mena cried out, excited again by this revelation of feeling.

"Oh God, yes," she sobbed.

Garrett increased his speed, riding toward his own horizon, and Mena wanted to see him find his pleasure. He looked at her from beneath his fallen curls as he thrust. Mena had never seen such a beautiful man before, and couldn't believe that he was here with her. She helplessly watched their bodies joining, mesmerized by his cock disappearing inside her.

Garrett growled, his head tossed back, and then he pulled out and spent into the sheets beside Mena on the bed. He collapsed forward, cradling her in his strong arms. She ran her fingers over his back, soothing him, feeling his sweat slicked muscles. After a moment, Garrett pushed up on his hands, and kissed her with an aching gentleness that nearly broke her heart.

Why had she ever refused him? She would sell her soul to the devil for another moment of this blinding pleasure.

"That was amazing," he said softly, stroking a finger along her jaw.

Mena blushed and smiled shyly.

"It was," she replied, and turned to press a kiss to his wrist.

"You have your own room, but if you want to stay here with me, I'd like that," he said, his tone hesitant.

Mena smiled, happy that her new husband wanted her close. It seemed only natural to lie side by side as they drifted off to sleep together. So far marriage had been a very good idea.

Twenty

The next morning Mena awoke to find Garrett missing. She threw a wrap over her night rail and went to find him. He was in the breakfast room reading the newspaper and absently chewing a piece of toast. He looked up over the edge of his paper when she entered, his eyes roving over her body in a way that made her heat.

"Good morning, wife," he said, voice low and rough with desire.

"Good morning," Mena responded, her face aflame as her mind conjured up images of their activities the night before.

She turned to the buffet and began to fill a plate with delectable food. This was pure heaven. And she didn't have to do so much as boil water. She took her plate to the table and sat opposite her husband. A thrill shot through her at that word: husband.

Quite ridiculous to be so excited over it, but she was. She picked up her fork and took a bite of coddled eggs. The taste was pure bliss. Garrett laid aside his newspaper and watched her eat for a moment.

"My mother is going to accompany us on the train this afternoon. I couldn't persuade her to give us our space, unfortunately, but it is a private car so at least we won't be too tightly packed on the journey," he said with a grimace as he took a sip of coffee.

Mena stared at him, frozen, fork suspended in air.

"What are you talking about?" she asked.

Garrett looked surprised.

"We are off to London this afternoon; I thought I told you that yesterday."

"No, you didn't," she said. "I do not want to go to London."

"It's a short journey," he said reasonably.

"That's hardly the point."

Her new husband sighed and leaned forward, bracing his elbows on the table.

"We have to go to London for the season, Philomena. I have to take my seat in the Lords and vote. It is my duty."

Mena arched a brow.

"I do take that duty seriously, your grace, but I shall not accompany you to London," she said calmly.

"Why the hell not?"

Mena was shocked by the outburst. She hadn't known Garrett to have a temper. But then, she didn't really know him at all, did she?

"I simply cannot," she replied.

Garrett leaned back in his chair and pushed his hands through his hair, sending the golden strands into disarray. He was so handsome it was difficult to argue rather than just kiss him into submission, but Mena refused to bend. She was nothing if not stubborn to a fault.

"So, I am to go away for weeks and not have my wife by my side? What would people think? I do not want to encourage ridiculous gossip," he said, and speared her with a sulky look.

Mena refused to be cowed. She could not face high society in London yet, especially not as a duchess. Garrett would have to go alone, or not at all. She rubbed her arms absently, as though to dispel a chill. She needed more time. Hadn't Garrett seen the way the others treated her at the party? It wouldn't be any better now.

"I absolutely refuse to go to London and be a part of that cesspool called society," she mumbled.

Mena had kept her voice low, merely grumbling her private thoughts, but Garrett had heard them and was instantly irate. Clearly, she had struck a nerve.

"I thought you understood that becoming my duchess would require certain performances, such as spending a little time in London," he sighed, running his hands fiercely through his hair. Mena worried that he was about to tug out large clumps of it in his fervor. "It's not like I'm a high-flying politician! We merely must put in a few appearances, and I have to cast some votes. But I do spend most of my time here, when I can."

He stared down at her, the power of his masculine frustration could be felt like a blow from across the table. Mena struggled to control her own rising temper, knowing full well that it did no good for them both to lose their composure.

"I was not aware, actually," she said, her words clipped. "I thought I had made it abundantly clear how little interest society holds for me."

She shrugged. Garrett's eyes narrowed to furious slits, and his nostrils flared.

"I see. I didn't realize that living in the literal lap of luxury was so awful for you."

"If you will recall, I never intended any of this," she pointed out.

"Then leave!" he shot back.

They both sat there, staring each other down. Where did they go from here? Mena struggled through her anger to think.

"I thought it was you who were leaving," she said finally, her tone cool.

Fuck it, she thought, this was her home and wealth now too.

With that she stood up and walked calmly from the room, leaving Garrett to stew.

***

Garrett let her go, then stood and stalked to the library and the soothing promise of his favorite chair and several glasses of good Scottish whiskey. He poured himself a tall glass, and then carried the rest of the bottle over to his chair. The fireplace was empty and the cool morning air blew into the room from the open terrace doors. He sighed in appreciation, enjoying the silent stillness of the moment. This was why it was foolish to marry. Once wed, a man never had a moment of peace to himself.

He held up his glass, about to take a drink, but stopped to consider the golden liquid. A feeling of melancholy swept over him. Perhaps he was missing Campbell. Garrett was glad for his friend's newfound happiness, but he missed his company.

Never mind—a man could be content alone. Indeed, it was a more natural state in which to exist. Much less complicated than close relationships. Garrett set his glass down without drinking. He stared blindly out into the garden, feeling regretful and lonely.

He needed to patch things up with his wife. He went upstairs where he found Mena's door ajar, spilling golden light across the carpet of their shared sitting room. He was helpless to resist his feet from bringing him toward it, like a moth drawn to flame.

Inside, Mena sat at her elegant little desk, writing. She looked so determined and focused that Garrett suspected this was something other than casual correspondence with a friend. He wanted to know what she was writing. He wanted to know her.

He knocked gently on the door, and Mena startled and turned.

"Can I help you?" she asked, holding herself stiffly with her bland mask firmly in place.

Garrett wanted her to relax and open up to him. He leaned on the doorframe and offered a little smile—the one that usually got women to forgive his indiscretions and welcome him back into their open arms.

"I'm sorry."

Her brows raised in surprise. Encouraged, he came closer. Mena visibly stiffened, and Garrett stopped. He didn't want to cause her to flee.

"I shouldn't have let my frustration get the better of me," he said, hands spread wide as he approached.

Mena blinked at him, then visibly softened, shifting in her seat to fully face him.

"Me either," she said ruefully. "I suppose I chafe at the very notion of someone telling me what to do."

Garrett smiled gently and sat on the edge of her bed.

"That I can understand, especially given what you've shared with me about your past. I don't much enjoy society either, as you know. We are fully in agreement that staying here is much preferable, but I'm trying to do right by my tenants and all who live in the village by casting my votes and paying some attention to the shenanigans in parliament. Maybe you could help me with that?"

It was an olive branch, but Garrett meant it. He was lost without Campbell to lend his ear about the estate, and Garrett had never been a good student, neither at Eton nor at his father's knee. Mena was intelligent, thoughtful, and a good listener. Surely, she would be a good partner in his work.

It was clearly the right thing to say, because she smiled broadly.

"I suppose I could," she allowed, chin lifted. "But promise me that you won't accept any invitations to large gatherings without consulting me. We must be partners. And no more surprise travel plans. I need time to adjust to…everything."

"Of course," he immediately agreed, relieved that their first fight was over so quickly.

Garrett leaned forward and held out a hand to her, willing her to come to him. She took his hand, allowing him to pull her close. As she stepped between his knees, she rested her hands on his shoulders and looked into his eyes.

"I'm not sorry that we married," she said softly.

Garrett's chest tightened with some unknown emotion, warmth spreading through him.

"I, for one, am glad that we did," he replied.

With a smile she leaned in and pressed a kiss to his lips. Garrett held still, allowing her to take the lead. Her mouth smoothed over his, her hands sliding up to encircle his neck as she sought to get closer. Garrett endured the erotic assault for as long as he could stand it before pulling her roughly into his lap with a growl and deepening the kiss. She responded passionately.

Yes, this marriage had been a very good idea, Garrett thought as they struggled out of their clothes, eager to feel each other's skin as they made love once more.

Chapter

Twenty-One

The dowager duchess sat in the shadows of the lavish train car, having dictated that the curtains must be closed to block out the sunshine. In her black crepe gown and elaborate veil, she looked like a vengeful ghost about to jump out to scare someone. Mena took a fortifying breath and stepped further into the room. She tried to smile brightly, but it didn't feel natural, and her face started to ache from the effort. Her dark gray traveling outfit rustled as she walked across the room to greet her new mother-in-law. She dipped a curtsy and stood before the woman.

"Good morning, your grace."

The older woman glowered, the wrinkled skin around her mouth adding to her sour expression a profusion of lines.

"We shall attend the opera tonight, and you are in dire need of instruction before then," she stated flatly.

Mena smothered the frustration that burned in her chest and kept her expression bland.

"Indeed? That sounds lovely. I've never attended before."

"Sit," the dowager commanded.

Mena took a seat opposite the dowager on one of the comfortable benches that lined the car, careful to tuck her skirts as she had been taught in finishing school, her back straight. The dowager did her best to be intimidating, but Mena had seen—and lived with—worse and she refused to be cowed. She held her chin high and looked the older woman in the eye. It was important not to show weakness, that was a mistake one didn't make more than once.

Mena had not been blessed with a loving mother, and her childhood had been fraught with the trauma of never being good enough. It was difficult to open herself up now to another potential mother figure; it left her feeling too exposed and vulnerable. Mena had struggled over the years to let her friends close, but now she had a flourishing collection of women who she had complete trust in.

But she still did not let down her guard easily, even with them. They all knew her to be a very private person. Having spent many years working at the orphanage Mena had also grown very close to Mrs. Farningham, the headmistress, who had come to be a sort of mother figure.

But now Mena had a new mother in her life, a tagalong to the new husband she had somehow gained. Mena would have preferred to ignore the older woman and live separate lives, but alas the dowager duchess intended to be...involved. Garrett and his sister, Lady Claire, clearly felt chafed by their mother's attentions and machinations, but did they truly dislike her? It did not appear so.

"Now, let us discuss your wardrobe," the dowager said with a disdainful sniff. "As we haven't had time to bring you to the dressmaker, we must make do with something else. Nothing I've seen you in will do, but you can likely fit into Claire's gowns, so I had a maid look through the attic storage and we have found an old one for you that will suit."

Mena took this in, holding herself with such tension that her neck and shoulders ached. So now her freedom of dress was to be taken from her.

"Thank you, your grace."

The dowager nodded.

"With the right corset, perhaps you will achieve the correct look."

The woman's grim expression left room for doubt on that matter, as her beady black eyes roamed over Mena's body, assessing her worth and finding her lacking. Mena bit her bottom lip until she tasted blood in an effort not to take the bait.

"Perhaps," Mena said tightly.

"Well, that's settled then. Now let us discuss how you shall be expected to behave."

Mena stiffened, her control hanging on by a thread.

"Have I done something to offend your grace?" she asked tightly.

Just then, Garrett entered the train car, with Lady Claire at his heels. As though he could sense the tense atmosphere, he said, "Are we getting along in here?"

Mena nodded, with as much confidence and grace as she could muster. She was but a boat floating along on the waves. Garrett bent to kiss his mother's cheek before taking a seat beside Mena, throwing his arm around her in a show of intimacy that caused Mena to blush. Claire took a seat on the bench opposite, and looked back and forth between Mena and the dowager, trying to ascertain their moods.

"Well, I know I am looking forward to seeing the city again. No offense, Garrett, but I find the country a bit tiresome," she said.

Once the train pulled into the station, they went out to the waiting carriage and were whisked off to the manor house the duke occupied during the season. It was a three-story mansion of cream-colored stone, like a miniature version of the estate house, with elaborately carved cornices that looked too delicate to withstand the poor English weather.

The drive featured twin lions carved from matching cream stone, reclining but watchful as the carriage pulled in. Mena took a deep breath, preparing herself for another onslaught of servant introductions before she could escape to her bedchamber.

Dinner was sent up to her room, and turned out to be a thin broth, tea, and a small bowl of sliced apples. Mena stared down at her dinner tray with a growing bonfire of anger rising within her. The old woman was trying to starve her, just as her own mother had. Mena had promised herself that this kind of hellish existence was behind her, but no matter how one tried to escape, expectation had a way of cramming you back into your place on the ladder of society.

When the maid arrived with the selected gown, an exhausted Mena was surprised to find it quite appealing. The dark wine-colored velvet was soft and luxurious. The cut of the gown was outdated, but it fit well, and Mena didn't want to extend any grace to her mother-in-law, but there were worse things than wearing something decently comfortable.

She stood in the center of her dressing room, her bare feet sinking into the thick Oriental carpet, waiting for another woman to help her dress as though she was a child. The crushing loneliness of her situation was starting to hit her. She knew no one in London, had a husband she barely knew, and a mother-in-law who was a grumpy curmudgeon.

Mena hugged herself and closed her eyes as she focused on breathing to avoid letting slip the tears that threatened to fall. She missed Buckinghamshire and her quiet life.

The maid clucked to herself as she tortured Mena's straight brown hair into a waterfall of curls that were gathered atop her head and then purposely disheveled. Pearl-tipped pins were placed strategically throughout the arrangement to wink in the light. As she tilted her head to consider it, Mena had to admit that it was beautiful. It took far too long for her taste, as she could think of a thousand better things to spend her time on, but it was nice to dress up like a princess for a day.

As she finally descended the stairs, Mena saw Garrett waiting in the foyer alongside the dowager, who was still frowning in all black garb. Garrett looked breathtakingly handsome in his evening attire, his golden hair curling over the top of his starched white collar. His eyes tracked her as Mena approached, and he seemed pleased with how she looked, which made Mena feel like a flower bud unfurling in the warm summer sun.

When she finally reached the bottom of the staircase, Mena stood awkwardly, twisting her gloved fingers together. Garrett stepped forward, and took one of her hands in his, warming her skin through the white silk of her elbow length gloves.

"Ready for the opera?" he asked, a playful smile tugging at his lips giving him a boyish look.

Mena nodded, but her stomach was a fist of anxiety. She wasn't entirely sure she could face the swarm of aristocrats that awaited her.

"You look lovely," Garrett said, his low tone unfurling a warmth in her belly, and he pressed a kiss to the back of her hand.

Mena felt her cheeks heat, even as she started shaking her head in denial.

"No, I don't, but thank you, regardless," she breathed.

"How I wish we could stay in all night, and I could prove your beauty to you, my dear, but alas…"

Garrett swept a glance over his shoulder toward his mother, who frowned in her black velvet gown, her white hair graced with three enormous swaying ostrich feathers dyed black, and a glittering diamond tiara.

"Don't be silly," Mena said absently, as she tried to smother the inferno of lust that threatened to melt her clothes off right there in the foyer.

"My son, ever the charmer," the dowager cut in with a disapproving tone. "We must be off now, Garrett, or we shall be late."

"It's fashionable to be late," he pointed out, winking conspiratorially at Mena before tucking her hand into the crook of his elbow.

"One can be unfashionably late," the dowager grumbled. "Especially if there is no one in the halls to see us come in. Why else go through all this trouble if not to have our gowns appreciated by the ton?"

Mena wanted to roll her eyes but felt another squeeze of anxiety in the pit of her empty stomach—she had been far too nervous to eat dinner.

"Quite right, Mother, as always," Garrett said soothingly, and led Mena to the door where the butler waited with their overcoats.

Garrett took Mena's cloak from the butler and slid it around her shoulders. The rough pad of his thumb slid along her collarbone, sending hot shivers of desire down her spine. Mena's breath caught and she wanted to melt back into his arms. She sternly reminded herself of the audience they had and pushed her lust aside for later.

"Is Lady Claire accompanying us?" she asked as they stepped through the front door to the awaiting carriage.

"Not this time. She has other plans, apparently," Garrett replied.

Once settled into the carriage, they were swept off through the dark city streets. Off on an adventure. Garrett squeezed Mena's hand, keeping hold of it. Mena watched the city through the window, focusing on her breath to keep the anxiety at bay.

Chapter

Twenty-Two

In front of the opera house carriages battled for position, each wanting to ensure their occupants arrived without having to step in a steaming pile of horse droppings. Ladies emerged, tall feathers flapping in the breeze from atop the mountain of hair they sported, jewels glimmering in the evening gaslight. As a duke, Garrett's carriage had no trouble forcing its way through to the very front door of the opera house, a liveried footman jumping down to hand them out.

As the crowd flowed into the opera house the excitement was palpable. The building dated back to 1808 when a fire destroyed much of the original building, and it had been rebuilt to resemble some kind of rather plain Roman temple design. But inside every inch was gilded and draped with elegant red velvet, the ceiling painted with cherubs and clouds gallivanting about the heavens.

Tonight, the music was German, and Mena was genuinely looking forward to hearing it. However, she was decidedly less enthused about the people she must contend with in order to hear it. She gripped Garrett's arm as they made their way through the crowd to their private box. Mena kept her gaze above any of the individuals, hoping to be spared their stares and judgment.

It was all too redolent of her finishing school days, with the sharp tongues ready to shred a girl for wearing the wrong color dress. The instructors had been just as vicious, armed with rulers to strike anyone who faltered during their curtsy or failed to maintain perfect posture on the stairs.

Mena tried to push away the dark memories bubbling up as she advanced through the foyer. Garrett's unwavering strength as he guided her along helped ease the tension in her shoulders. As long as he was beside her, she could face anything.

The dowager trailed behind, assisted by a handsome young footman. As a well-known member of the most elite circles, she attracted plenty of appreciative glances from the ladies, and the dowager seemed pleased to be the subject of so much attention.

They made their way to the duke's private box which boasted one of the best views of the stage, complete with a row of neatly arranged chairs. Garrett helped Mena into her seat before claiming the one beside her; the dowager's footman escort stood behind his charge, hands clasped behind his back.

Garrett handed Mena a pair of brass opera glasses.

"Tonight, the show is Hansel and Gretel by Strauss, and I hear it is highly entertaining."

The lights dimmed just then, and the orchestra struck the opening notes. Mena leaned forward, eager to see what would happen. The thick red curtains parted, and her senses were assaulted with the sweetest music and colorful costumes of the players. It was such fun, she found herself quite lost in the performance.

Eventually it was time for intermission, and the lights were turned up again to illuminate the way for theatergoers to find their way to the refreshment tables.

"It is usual for people to visit between boxes," Garrett leaned in to warn her seconds before the curtain was pulled back to allow a crush of people to enter the box.

Garrett stood to greet their visitors. The dowager remained seated, so Mena did as well.

"May I present my wife, Duchess Philomena Bedford."

Several pairs of critical eyes turned to her, and Mena had to remind herself to not tremble under their scrutiny. She was *their* social better now. The thought brought a tiny smile to her lips as the toffs were forced to bow and scrape before her despite their obvious reticence.

"Wonderful to meet you all," she said with a slight incline of her head.

"How are you finding London, your grace?" one of the gentlemen asked with a knowing smile.

"We have just arrived today, but I am enjoying the opera immensely," Mena replied.

He appeared disappointed to not have unsettled her with that question. Did everyone know her humble origins, then?

"You simply must come to the soiree," someone was chattering.

It was difficult to follow the flow of conversation with so many people crammed into the limited box space. The air was growing hot, and Mena longed for escape, or at least a cool drink. But none of the other ladies were partaking, which meant she must go without as well. And here she'd thought ladies were fragile and in need of tender care. Yet their needs went not only unmet but unasked as well.

One of the ladies wore a dress so tight to her lush curves that Mena almost blushed to see it. The lady clearly knew it was an attention grabber, and she happily flaunted her body and the effect it had on the men in particular. Mena found herself struggling with a ridiculous emotion—jealousy. She tried to covertly study Garrett to see how he reacted, but he appeared not to notice the woman at all, much to Mena's pleasure.

The dowager leaned in to speak quietly to Mena.

"It is usual for politics to intrude on our leisure time. Best to let the men get on with it privately or else we'll never have a moment's peace."

Apparently, it was customary for the men to depart for the smoking lounge where they could get a moment away from their women and indulge in some general buffoonery. Mena just had to make it until midnight and then she would be on her way home, and ready for a fortifying meal—her stomach was still rumbling from lack of proper nourishment.

Mena watched her husband leave, along with several of the men present. The ladies continued to hover, eager for scraps of gossip for sharing later. One of them drifted over to sit by Mena.

"Good evening, your grace. It is good to make your acquaintance."

"You as well, Lady…"

"Lady Crane," the woman helpfully supplied.

"How are you enjoying the opera?" Mena asked, doing her best to engage in the polite discussion required of someone in her position.

Lady Crane looked toward the stage, an unmistakable expression of sadness flickering across her face before being carefully concealed.

"I have seen this one before, and it is indeed a favorite," she said, then turned to look into Mena's eyes. "But I really came to see you."

"Oh?" Mena croaked out, unsure of what that meant.

"Yes, I knew you would be the right person to speak with about—" Lady Crane began, then cut herself off before looking around them. She lowered her voice. "I need your help, you see."

Mena looked into the other woman's emerald eyes, shining with unspent emotion. Her heart constricted in her chest, feeling the other woman's pain. But she was also on guard, all too aware of the danger inherent in her work. If she trusted the wrong person, many lives would be ruined.

"What do you need help with, my lady?" she asked carefully.

The other woman took a deep breath, indecision flashing across her features before she shook her head slightly.

"My modiste told me of a network that helps women in need," she said, keeping her voice low.

Mena's heart pounded, alarm bells ringing in her ears.

"Is that so?"

Lady Crane nodded, eyes grave. "She told me a secret to give to the new duchess. Mother Earth."

Relief coursed through her, as the code for friends to identify each other fell from the other woman's lips. Mena could trust her, but that did not mean the danger was over. In many ways, the danger had just begun to make itself known.

"I am always here to help," she murmured, and reached into her reticule for one of the cards she carried everywhere. "Please come for a visit soon."

She handed the card discreetly to Lady Crane, who took it without even glancing at it and slid it into a secret pocket of her gown. Her delicate cheeks flushed pink.

"Thank you, your grace. I shall. If you will excuse me."

She stood and fled from the box. Mena watched her go, hoping that the lady would be safe tonight, from whatever it was she feared.

***

In the men's lounge the air was thick with cigar smoke and the smell of pomade. Garrett longed to return to his box, and to his bride. He found himself enthralled by her reaction to the opera, her breathy laughs of delight and soft gasps of sorrow far more interesting that the performance itself. But unfortunately, Garrett was trapped here with the men.

"Your grace, you must vote with the Conservatives this session or else the Liberals will take back the position of Prime Minister. The queen is most anxious," Viscount Bently Pickering said, eyes overbright from the wine he was liberally drinking as though the theater were about to run out.

"And what of the growing Labor party? They've been holding meetings and rumor is they might soon be able to snag some seats in the Commons," Garrett pointed out. "Seems to me you should be considering a coalition with the Liberal faction to ward off this working class menace."

"Keir Hardie is trying to formalize a coalition with the Scots, and I fear the Liberals might throw their lot in with them."

"Why should they? The Liberals are ultimately more aligned with the interests of the upper classes," Garrett said, waving off the other man's anxiety.

"Yes, it's very concerning. It's as if these people want to see this great country destroyed," Pickering slurred, his complexion growing red.

"You don't think the Liberals can keep the working class contained? They have done well so far, even with the Socialists mobilizing support across the continent," Garrett shrugged.

"Ever the voice of calm, your grace," the other man said as he smiled coldly. "But no. The great unwashed masses are rising up through the cracks like spring mud, no matter how well we try to hold them in line."

Garrett sipped his drink, wondering what Mena would think. Inwardly he smiled, knowing that his wife would be standing up for the "great unwashed" peoples, and she would have the right of it.

"Well, Bently, you've certainly given me something to consider," he said pleasantly.

While a duke might throw his weight around, it hadn't been Garrett's style to do so. He wasn't a leader. But he was stayed from leaving by the other man's hand on his shoulder.

"Your grace, the empire is dealing with great turbulence abroad. We need to keep things settled at home. We cannot afford another farming debacle. So many peers have yet to recover, and some are resorting to marrying American heiresses, if one can imagine," he said with a grimace—the very idea! "Women are wearing trousers in the street for God's sake."

Garrett resisted rolling his eyes—as if women wearing trousers was some evidence of debauchery. Certainly, it was better for all if ladies were free to travel about by bicycle, and trousers were safer for such an activity than the restrictive layers of traditional heavy skirts.

"I am sure we can continue to improve the lives of British peoples without causing the whole of the country to burn down. Don't you agree?" he said with a laugh.

The other man looked skeptical but was prevented from responding by the signal to return to their seats for the show.

Garrett clapped Pickering on the back, finished his drink and put it on a passing footman's tray as he made his way out of the gentlemen's lounge.

As he turned the corner, Garrett found himself watching Lord Beckwith coming down the hall. The other man met his eye steadily as he advanced. Wonderful. All Garrett wanted to do was return to Mena, and now he was going to be stuck talking to Beckwith of all people.

"Evening, Bedford."

Garrett gritted his teeth, determined to continue on his way. He managed a curt nod in response before passing the other man, never slowing his pace. It was certainly rude, but Garrett brushed off the instinct to worry over Beckwith's opinion on the matter. The man hardly warranted concern about his feelings. Blessedly, that was the end of the interaction, and Garrett made a clean escape.

Once back at the family box, which was blessedly empty but for Mena and his mother, Garrett slid into his seat and reached out to take Mena's gloved hand in his. She looked over at him in surprise, but her lips curved into a smile as they regarded each other. The music drifted to their ears as the orchestra began to play again, and the show continued on.

Chapter

Twenty-Three

Lady Crane sat on the edge of her chair, back straighter than a fence post, trembling hands clutching her teacup in Mena's sitting room. Her green eyes shimmered with sadness.

"I was very young, barely eighteen, when we wed. I hardly got a taste of my first season," she said as she shook her head miserably, chin lowered to brush the stiff lace collar of her expensive visiting gown.

"Is he cruel?" Mena asked as gently as she could.

Lady Crane nodded, the movement so small that one could almost miss it if they weren't watching closely. She took a steadying breath before she raised her head and said, "Clarence is very demanding. I didn't mind when it was just about my wardrobe and menus. But over time it got worse. He flies into a rage at the slightest thing now..." She trailed off, her eyes trained on the carpet.

Mena leaned forward to place her hand on the other woman's shoulder for comfort.

"You don't have to tell me anything more, unless you wish to. I am here to listen, but no matter what you say, no one should be controlled by another. Women need not live their lives under the thumb of any man. So, no matter your reasons, I will help you."

Lady Crane turned her gaze to Mena, eyes glistening with tears. She nodded as her chin trembled with emotion.

"Thank you, your grace. I knew you were the person to turn to," she said, before wiping a tear from the corner of her eye. "Clarence started controlling who I was able to meet and speak with last year, and has only grown more jealous over time. He is enraged that I have not produced an heir yet," her voice snagged, and she had to pause for a breath, swallowing audibly. "I don't mind that he keeps a mistress. In fact, it is a relief. But he hit me the day before the opera where we spoke."

She paused to elegantly press a handkerchief to her nose, squeezing her eyes shut with a moan, struggling to contain her sorrow.

"I was so shocked...it never occurred to me that he could be violent. I didn't know what to do, but I had heard things...heard that you were connected with Lady Lytton and others. I don't mean to put you to any trouble—"

"No, put that out of your mind," Mena said, cutting the other woman off. "I want to help you. What else should a duchess do with her position than help others?" Mena was vehement in her refusal to turn away a woman in need.

"Thank you, I am just so thankful, your grace."

"Call me Mena, please. Now, what would you like to do first? Do you wish to return home to collect anything? Or are you wanting to leave right away? I know a place you can stay while we get tickets for you to go abroad."

Lady Crane sniffled and dabbed her eyes.

"I have no living family, I'm afraid. But I cannot leave with nothing…I won't allow that man the satisfaction." Her chin lifted in defiance. "I should pack some valuables for sale later. Lord Crane is scheduled to be away on business in Scotland next month, and will be gone for several weeks."

Mena nodded, thinking.

"Alright, good. I suggest we make sure you are gone by the second day he is gone at the latest. That gives us plenty of time to get you out of the country. Will you be able to get your affairs in order by then?"

Lady Crane nodded slowly.

"Yes, I think so. Can I impose upon you to send a carriage for me on the day? I don't want to take a hack, nor can I take one of my husband's carriages. I don't wish to hang for horse thievery," she said with a laugh that bordered on hysterical.

Mena patted her shoulder soothingly.

"Yes of course. I will come collect you myself. Is there anything else I can help you with?"

"No, thank you, your grace. I'm so relieved to know this nightmare will soon be over," Lady Crane said as she stood and smoothed her skirts.

Mena led her guest out, making sure to see her safely tucked into a hack before returning to the house. She collapsed into her chair with a sigh. Some part of her worried that Garrett would be upset to find out about this secret work of hers, stealing the wives of wealthy powerful men from beneath their noses—effectively thievery of property, according to the law.

She could be jailed for such activity. And Garrett could either support her, shielding her from consequences, or be the one to toss her to the wolves. Mena put a hand to the back of her neck, rubbing to try and relieve the tension gathering there. She didn't know what to do—tell him, or not?

* * *

The weeks had been passing happily, Mena immersed in marital bliss and Garrett pursuing his political responsibilities for the first time. They got on well, attended events together, and spent their evenings in passion-fueled oblivion.

Mena chewed on the end of her pencil, deep in thought, imagining trailing her fingers along the veins on Garrett's fore-arms, lingering over the muscles that bunched and moved as he wrote. She had to physically shake herself out of the daydream and return her attention to her letters. This was why she hadn't been after marrying—it got in the way of important work.

Mena had recently begun corresponding with some American suffragettes and found them endlessly entertaining. They were also fond of animals, so it was an easy friendship to develop. Mena hoped to someday visit America. She supposed that was yet another good quality duchesses possess—the time and finances for international travel.

Currently Mena was assisting Lady Constance Lytton with organizing a group of women for a rally in London, and she still had to speak to Clem's father, Doctor Blakely, regarding an effec-tive birth control agent. Women would never be truly free unless they could control how and when they reproduced.

This was the kind of behavior that could see her arrested. However, now that she was a duchess, that seemed far less likely. Especially if she had her husband's support. Mena flicked a glance over at Garrett who was studying the paper like it was very important.

"Deeds, not words" Mena wrote at the bottom of the let-ter she was writing, then smiled softly to herself. She was not fond of public speaking, but she knew how to help the cause in her own way. Mena was instrumental in connecting young women just emerging into the world again from the confines of the finishing school with active suffragette societies. She was a shepherdess leading young women to freedom, including Lady Crane, who was eager to escape her prison of a marriage at the first opportunity. Mena hoped to provide the path to independence.

But it was very secretive work, and one that could create enemies. Not even Thalia and Clementine knew about this. Thalia was busy with her confectionary shop, and now her new husband, so it wasn't difficult to avoid the subject. But Clem was a bloody good journalist and activist, and with her connections Mena was certain the truth would come out eventually. So far it had not. Mena was fairly certain her closest friends did suspect something, though they'd never asked.

"Would you like some tea?" Garrett asked, causing Mena to jolt out of her musings.

"Oh, yes, thank you," Mena managed, setting her pencil down.

Garrett poured a stream of steaming tea into a cup, adding just the right amount of cream, and then brought the cup to her. Men typically did not pour tea, nor did they care to know the particular tea habits of those around them; not in the way women were raised to obsess over every detail to prove their worth. It was yet another reminder of how unique her husband was.

Mena took the cup, beaming at her husband like a lovestruck fool. She found herself unable to temper her enthusiasm for him, despite her worry over how that reflected on her.

Garrett had a twinkle in his eye and was fairly bouncing on his heels with excitement.

"I have something for you," he said.

"Is that so?" she asked, sipping her tea.

Mena shook her head with a rueful smile, unsure of what kind of surprise awaited her. Garrett drew her over to a basket sitting on the floor. Suddenly the basket wiggled, and the top popped open to reveal a furry brown and white spotted head.

"Oh, my lord, you didn't!" Mena cried, pressing her hands to her cheeks.

"Oh, but I did, come see," Garrett replied with a laugh.

Mena rushed to the basket, and scooped the wiggling puppy up into her arms, burying her face in its warm fuzz. It smelled like heaven. Her eyes were misty as she looked up at her husband.

"Thank you so much. I have missed my dog so much since we came to London. He was far too old to journey about the country," she said, melancholy burning in her chest.

"I suspected so, and you're welcome," he said with an easy smile, his hands in his trouser pockets. "Soon enough we will travel back, and you will be able to see Gruff again."

Mena nodded, grateful for Garrett's sensitivity and attention to detail. She snuggled the new puppy to her chest, letting its warmth soothe her.

"I love him, and you," Mena said.

Garrett stilled, expression tense.

"Uh…"

Mena realized her mistake, and shot to her feet, cradling the puppy to her chest like some sort of flimsy shield.

"I mean…I love that you bought him for me, it's very sweet and it means so much to me," she corrected awkwardly.

They considered each other warily, each waiting for the other to speak, their eyes locked. Mena broke the connection, dragged in a shuddering breath, and placed the puppy gently back into its basket.

She crossed the room to Garrett, stopping inches from him, her chin tilted up so she could look into his eyes. Garrett held his breath, waiting for her move. Mena reached up and touched his chest, placing her palm over his heart, feeling his strong muscles flex beneath her burning touch. A coy smile curved her lips. Garrett was drawn to her, unable to hold back from seizing her mouth in a scorching kiss. Her lips parted on a sigh, and the kiss deepened, their tongues tangling.

They shed their clothing as quickly as possible, dropping items as they slowly kissed their way across the room to the bed. Garrett was naked, his skin gleaming in the flickering light from the fireplace. He helped Mena out of her gown and corset, dropping them to the floor. They reached for each other, and fell back on the settee while kissing, Garrett's hands buried in her shining chestnut hair. He cradled her head in one of his large hands, using his other to ease her chemise down, baring the sensitive skin of her shoulder. A shiver raced down her spine as the cool air caused goosebumps to spread across her naked flesh. His mouth dragged down her jaw, along her throat, and he paused to gently suckle her downy skin, leaving a love bruise in the crook of her neck and shoulder where her collarbone jutted out.

Mena moaned, pressing herself closer against his hard body, needing his touch, drawn like a moth to flame. Garrett growled in response and tilted his hips to grind his throbbing cock into her lower belly. They were reduced to animal communication, feral and earthy in this connection.

Suddenly he tore the rest of the thin fabric from her body, and his hands claimed her flesh, gripping her buttocks as he took her mouth in a hot possessive kiss, his tongue thrusting into her mouth in a crude approximation of his future intent. Mena was lost to the moment, a creature of pure need and sensation. Her quim throbbed with need, slick heat begging for attention. She knew how good he felt, and she was greedy for it.

She tore her lips from his and held his face between her hands, forcing him to look into her eyes.

"I need you, Garrett. Take me," she commanded.

His pupils dilated, a muscle ticking in his jaw. He had the wild look of a predator about to close in on its prey. He slipped his arms under her, lifting her body easily and brought her to the immense bed. She was tossed upon the counterpane, eliciting a wild squeal of delight from her throat. Mena flipped over to her back, and let her legs fall open as she speared him with a commanding look. She felt feral and free in her lust. What power. She felt drunk on it.

"Come here," she demanded, crooking a finger at her husband.

"You drive me wild, my duchess," he said, voice low and growly with his desire.

"Show me."

He stalked to the bed and crawled across to reach her, settling over her with panther-like grace. His cock pressed into her wet heat, but he stalled, drawing out her lust, punishing her for greed. Mena slid her hands down his back, feeling the angles of his muscles bunching and flexing. What luck that such a man was between her thighs, ready to satisfy her desires until she begged him to come. She raked her fingernails

down over his buttocks. Garrett threw his head back with a groan.

"You minx. I want to take this slow for you."

Mena smiled.

"I don't want slow. I want hard and fast."

He stared down at her, eyes wide in surprise at her audacity. But his cock pulsed against her heat, demanding to give them what they both wanted.

He slid inside, spearing her with a hard thrust that buried him to the hilt. Mena cried out, loving the roughness of the action.

"Yes!"

Garrett growled, words lost. He held her thighs open, allowing him to reach deeper as he thrust into her body, giving her waves of pleasure that built until her orgasm loomed, so fast, so soon. Her quim clenched him tightly, as she rocketed over the edge into delicious oblivion.

Holding her, he flipped over, settling Mena onto his lap with her legs astride his powerful thighs. She rode him.

Garrett continued to thrust up into her body as she came apart again, until he soon was calling her name as he too found his pleasure.

"I love you," she whispered, face pressed into his shoulder as he shattered in her arms.

Love had crept up on her unexpectedly, growing quietly without her notice. But that was the truth of it. Perhaps she had loved him from the first moment he had noticed her, treating her with respect from the start.

After, they lay together, slick with sweat, as their breathing slowed.

"That was...something," he said with a lopsided grin.

Mena turned her head to look at him, and laughed.

"Yes, it certainly was."

After fetching some cloth to clean them both up, Garrett stretched out on the bed, settling her against him, back to front. Mena drifted off to sleep, feeling the slow beating of his heart against her, reminding her that she was safe, and she dared to hope for his love in return. Perhaps someday he would give her his heart.

Chapter

Twenty-Four

The next afternoon, Mena descended the grand staircase and made her way to the family parlor. She needed to know if she was to be expected somewhere this afternoon or evening—it was a good day to meet with Lady Crane and plan an escape. She would need some money and a carriage, but that shouldn't be too difficult.

Mena called for a footman and was startled when her own father strolled in behind the butler.

"Excuse me, your grace, but Sir Harvey-Morton has arrived. Shall I fetch tea?"

Mena blinked.

"Uh, yes, thank you Stevens. Hello, Father, how are you?" she asked, coming forward to embrace her father.

He hugged her tightly, and then held onto her shoulders to look her over.

"You look wonderful, Philomena. I see that marriage agrees with you," Sir Harvey-Morton exclaimed happily, then released her to claim a seat in one of the comfortable chairs.

Mena sat on the settee.

"We have been quite happy, yes. What brings you to London?"

"Well, I came to see you, my dear," he answered with a smile. "But I am also attending a gathering of church leaders."

Mena nodded, though some instinct was causing her unease. Stevens, the butler of their London residence, returned then with the tea tray, and settled it upon the low table between Mena and her father before quietly leaving again. Mena poured out the tea and handed her father his cup.

"Well, I'm glad you stopped over for a visit," she said carefully, taking a sip of tea. "Garrett took me to the opera the first evening after we arrived. It was a wonderful experience. Perhaps if you have time you could come with us to another show. Or at least come for dinner."

"I shall try my best to make the time. You know I would love to meet your new family. And you can thank me for your marriage, of course," her father smiled.

Mena gaped at her father, feeling the world tilt sickeningly.

"What do you mean?" she gasped, fighting the instinct to scream out in alarm.

Her throat ached from the effort it took to hold back the sound.

Sir Harvey-Morton frowned at her impatiently.

"Now don't get hysterical, my dear. What I did was for your best interest; and look—now you're happily married to the illustrious duke of Bedford! Attending the opera and such."

Mena shook her head slowly, struggling to make sense of what she was hearing.

"It was you? But...how?"

Her father puffed his chest with pride, a grin spreading across his wide face.

"I wasn't certain it would work, of course. But it was worth a chance. I'd seen how you two were looking at each other, and when you both came in wet from the rain, I had my suspicions. So that night when you slipped out together to the library, I simply waited a few minutes before suggesting the countess might like a certain book, and voila!" He spread his hands wide like a showman.

Mena felt sick. She clutched the cushioned armrest, needing something solid to cling to. Breathe, just breathe, she commanded herself, but as she wheezed it was hard to keep herself from panicking. She looked up at her father, pinning him with an accusing glare.

"How was this in my interest?"

Her father shrugged, suddenly unwilling to meet her eyes. "Well, you know how things are back home."

Mena's eyes narrowed. "You mean financially?" she asked.

"Of course," came the reply, as her father spread his hands wide and plastered on a plaintive sort of smile. "Your duke really helped ease the stress I've been carrying."

"By easing your debts, I suppose."

Sir Harvey-Morton's smile turned sheepish, but he didn't deny her accusation. Anger bubbled up in Mena's chest as she blinked at the man who had raised her—the man who claimed to speak for God and stand for all that was good and just. He had been exposed for the charlatan he was, and it filled Mena with righteous fury.

"Don't you realize what this means? Garrett will think I'm a manipulative liar. The trust will be broken. You've ruined everything," she gritted out through clenched teeth.

Sir Harvey-Morton scoffed with a wave of his hand.

"Don't be ridiculous. He doesn't need to know."

Brows raised in wonder, she said, "It is you who are utterly ignorant in this, father. I cannot keep this from my husband. Nor am I giving you money, which I assume you've come to demand."

"Now Philomena, you know very well I have not asked for a penny from you," her father answered, putting on the false piety he wore so well before his congregation.

"Tell me you aren't here to ask for money," Mena said, challenging him to say the words.

He blinked at her in confusion for a moment, before his brows settled into a fierce scowl. But it seemed he was out of excuses for now.

"It is not demanding to request a little support from my only daughter," he said evenly.

Mena sighed, balling her fists in her lap to keep from throwing the teapot across the room. Her hands trembled in her lap, and she balled them into tight fists. It was important to stay composed. No one took an emotional woman seriously, not even a supposedly loving and concerned father.

"I will not give you one penny, father."

The words were out now. Mena could hardly keep from jumping to her feet to pace the room. Her entire body felt the ripple of electric discomfort from staring down her father, who looked about ready to explode.

"You will if you know what's good for you," her father said, with an indignant huff as his cheeks flushed red. "I could be tossed out on my ear, and you could be exiled and penniless."

Mena swallowed, struggling to clear the dry lump from her throat. He was right, of course. What could she do to prevent Garrett from punishing her and her arrogantly stupid father? Legally nothing, but she knew Garrett to be a good man...she loved him.

Misery constricted her heart. She didn't want to keep a secret like this and lie to him day after day. But they were happy, and she was loath to do anything to endanger the fragile connection they were building.

"Get out, father. I don't want to see you for a while," she said wearily, feeling suddenly exhausted by the whole situation.

He frowned at her, but sighed and set down his teacup and bid her good day, pressing a moist kiss to her cheek.

"Come see me when you decide to move past this," he said as he swept out the door, head held high as though he hadn't just shattered her entire world.

Taking a shaky breath, Mena slid her hands down her skirts, self-soothing as her mind frantically worked through scenarios. What should she do? She stared at the rapidly cooling tea and biscuits that sat untouched, feeling desolate.

The clock ticked away across the room, and Mena knew she wasn't capable of giving Lady Crane the type of level-headed support she needed. They would have to postpone the escape.

What a fucking mess.

* * *

"Rumor has it, Bedford, that you are saddled with some low born wife." Lord Bronnington sneered at Garrett as he delivered this bit of gossip, his voice loud enough to carry across the crowded club where men from the House of Lords gathered before the votes.

Garrett kept his expression impassive, refusing to grant the other man the display of emotion that he clearly desired. What occurred in his marriage was no one else's business. Garrett viciously stuffed down his simmering rage. He refused to give this man any ammunition in his quest. Garrett needed to speak to his wife.

"My wife is from Buckinghamshire," he replied carefully, keeping himself tightly in check.

Bronnington skewered him with an assessing look, eager to suss out the truth of the situation.

"A vicar's daughter, is that right?" he persisted.

Garrett's jaw clenched, and he spoke through his teeth, "Yes."

"Ah, well I would have assumed she was a great beauty, but I've rather heard differently," Bronnington chuckled.

It took all of Garrett's control not to punch the other man in the face. His knuckles tightened around his whiskey glass, but he managed to keep himself on the leash.

"Watch your next words very carefully, Bronnington," he warned with a hard look.

"Ah come on, Bedford. I'm just riling you up, don't worry. It's not like you had the duty to secure a wealthy heiress like the rest of us poor sods. She must make you happy, and that's what matters."

Garrett relaxed a bit, but it bothered him that people were talking—possibly laughing—about Mena behind her back. He had brought her into this world, and he refused to sit by and allow it to eat her alive.

When he arrived back home later, Mena was in the library at her desk, furiously writing. Garrett paused to watch her, pen moving across the page with the speed of an irate stallion, her brow furrowed in concentration. She wore a new dinner gown, no doubt purchased under the direction of the dowager, and it suited her.

"Good evening," Garrett said as he strolled inside the room.

Mena startled and set down her pen with great care before rising to her feet. She avoided his gaze.

"We need to speak about something that happened today at Parliament. A rumor is making the rounds...a rumor that you happen to be the main target of."

Her eyes shot to his, wide with alarm.

"What is it?" she asked, an edge to her voice.

"I suspect some bitter house guests of mine are delighting in spreading gossip about your class," he said.

Mena looked relieved, which puzzled him.

"I thought that would bother you," he said hesitantly.

She shifted her weight between her two feet, eyes fixed on a distant corner rather than him.

"I was worried it was something else. I...may have been engaged in illegal behavior."

She swallowed, and finally met his eyes.

He looked thoroughly confused now. "What kind of behavior?"

Mena took a deep breath. "I have helped several women leave their abusive marriages, including some very prominent ones."

"Okay...why though?"

"I had to," she explained, gesturing with her hands. "If a woman wanted to leave her marriage, and her husband was stopping her from doing so, I would help get her to safety and start a new life." She finished with a slight shrug.

"And did you stop to think about how powerful her husband might be?"

"That is entirely the point," she said, frowning. "She had no way of escape, and he was threatening to have her committed. Do you know what they do to women in those asylums?"

Her eyes were wide with the horror of it. Garrett didn't know, but he wasn't sure he wanted to, based on Mena's reaction. He ran a hand through his hair in frustration, sending the curling locks into disarray.

"I don't understand why you didn't tell me. What did you think I would do?"

Mena stood still, her back straight as an iron rod, her chin lifted in defiance, though her eyes were anxious.

"What most men would do," she answered, carefully enunciating each word.

Garrett blew out a breath.

"I am not most men, Philomena." He stalked to the fireplace, picked up the heavy poker and started jabbing at the fire.

Mena watched him warily, but stubbornly refused to move an inch.

"Just please hear this," Garrett said, forcing his voice to be gentle. "I support you, and I care about your interests. I want you to confide in me."

He didn't turn his head to see her reaction, but let the dancing flames before him soothe his wounded ego. Soft footsteps approached, and he felt a hand on his shoulder tentatively resting on him, searing his flesh with its warmth. Garrett turned to look at her. Mena looked past him, absorbed in the movement of the flames behind the grate.

"I am not used to having a confidante. Not even Thalia and Clem know the truth of it," she admitted in a quiet voice.

"You can trust me, Mena," Garrett said firmly.

She nodded slightly, still avoiding his gaze. After a moment of comfortable silence between them, she spoke again.

"I thought you might be angry..."

"No, just hurt that you didn't share this with me. I am here to help you bear your burdens, not increase the load."

Mena looked at him then, her dark eyes reflecting the firelight made the hair on the back of his neck stand up. She was a goddess, all strength and fire and energy, ready to change the world. She studied his face, focused and intent, roaming his features as though committing them to memory. Garrett's heart rate picked up, thumping in his throat and making his blood sing.

Something in her gaze answered a silent plea from his own soul. Love.

No, surely not that, how ridiculous. Their marriage was not based in love, just convenience and a strong current of lust. Love was not something Garrett would have in his life, and that was fine by him. It led to nothing positive, and only left one open to pain and loss.

"Can we sit and discuss this then?" she asked, tearing her gaze away.

Garrett replaced the poker and threw himself into a wing-back chair with Mena taking the chair opposite.

She twisted her fingers together in her lap, though her face remained stoic. If one didn't know her at all, they would assume she was perfectly calm. Garrett wished he could ease her anxiety.

"Perhaps we should have a drink," he offered, and stood to make his way to the sideboard where a selection of crystal decanters and glasses awaited, along with a bowl of fresh ice and chilled fruit.

The staff certainly knew his habits, but Garrett always felt a hit of guilt and self-loathing when he was reminded of his drink obsession. Maybe he should limit himself more, especially now that he was married and sharing his life with someone who depended on him. He pushed those thoughts aside as he filled two glasses with a finger of whiskey each and carried them back to his seat. He handed one to Mena, which she warmed with her hands, and he sipped his own, needing the soothing burn.

Finally, Mena took a small sip of her whiskey, grimaced, and then began to speak.

"It began while I was away at school," she started slowly. "It was terrible, and that may sound dramatic, but it really was a terrible experience. We had no agency, no freedom at all, and physically it was difficult as well. They denied us food, starving us until our waists were deemed an acceptable size. The corseting made it almost impossible to breathe, and yet we were forced to perform hours of activity, like dancing. We spent so much time pouring tea and curtsying I could scream."

She shook her head with a rueful smile. "Some of the girls took to it like a duck to water, a natural fit. But some of us...we struggled. It has never been in my nature to take such instruction easily. And then there was my roommate, Ashley. She really couldn't stand it, and even self-harmed."

She looked down at her hands, and bit her lower lip hard to stave off the threatening tears. She took a deep breath, and slowly released it, before continuing.

"At my lowest point a new teacher came to the school to take over our Latin instruction. She gave me a lifeline by slipping me a copy of Mary Wallenstonecraft's seminal work and inside was an address of a woman for me to write to. It was Lady Merideth Montgomery. Ever since that first letter, we've kept in touch, and I help send girls her way who are in need of guidance and support."

"And this is what you have hidden from everyone? What is wrong with that?"

"You don't understand the danger in this work. Women are routinely imprisoned, force fed with rubber tubes, beaten by the police, thrown from their homes and jobs. The power that refuses women the vote and equal rights will stop at nothing to end the movement. We are all in danger, and now that you know...you are a liability and in danger yourself."

Garrett snorted.

"I'm the Duke of Bedford. I am untouchable."

"No one is untouchable," she said solemnly, and Garrett wondered at her words.

"Honestly, I'm bloody jealous of you."

Her head jerked up in surprise. "What… why?"

"Because you have a passion, something that gives back to the world, changes it for the better. I don't have that."

"You have the tenants and so many others that benefit from the dukedom," she pointed out.

Garrett laughed bitterly.

"Ah yes, the dukedom." He paused to throw back the remainder of his drink. "It doesn't strike me as fair that some babies are born titled and powerful, while the majority are born into impoverished arms. Why me? What makes me worthy?" He looked up at Mena and caught her sympathetic gaze before looking away quickly. "I don't deserve this life, I haven't earned anything. I am only now getting my bearings as a landowner, thanks to Campbell's hard work. Hiring him to manage my estate got things in order and resulted in happy tenants. Highly productive, too. When he left to marry Thalia, the responsibility became mine again, and I realized the enormity of the effort required to keep it all going. So, what do I have to be proud of?"

He shook his head, defeated.

Mena slid from her chair to the floor, kneeling before Garrett, her hands on his knees as she willed him to look at her.

"You are worthy, Garrett, and you will find something that brings you pride and joy and fulfillment. Do not despair."

From her position on her knees, Garrett's perverted mind immediately went to what she could be doing from there. Unbidden, an image flashed in his mind of her mouth on him, licking and sucking as he filled her. He shook his head to rid himself of that image. But something in her expression made him think that she shared his thought.

Her hands slid up from his knees, excruciatingly slowly up toward the buttons that kept his trousers closed. She stroked him through the woolen fabric, instantly sending him over the edge.

"What are you doing?" he asked, his voice sounding strangled in his throat.

She laughed softly as she released his cock from the prison of his trousers. Garrett hissed as her hands encircled the length of him and squeezed. He closed his eyes in a slow blink, fingers digging into his chair, and then she thoroughly surprised him. Her lips curled around the tip of his cock, sending electric jolts of lust through him, flexing his thighs beneath her delicate hands.

"Wait, you don't have to..."

He left off speaking as she moved to take more of him in her luscious mouth. It was too much for Garrett to resist. His head fell back against the back of his chair, letting it support him as pleasure wracked his entire being. She moaned softly as she took him deep, sliding up and down his length with enthusiasm.

At the last moment, she looked up at him. Their eyes met as she suckled, and Garrett fell over the edge into the pleasurable abyss as his orgasm shook him. He looked at Mena in wonder. He couldn't believe how amazing she was.

Chapter
Twenty-Five

In the dark of the night, Garrett crept down to the kitchen for a midnight snack. Love making with his wife sapped his energy and left him famished. On his way back, scone in hand, he was startled to find his sister in the hall.

"What are you doing?" he demanded in a hushed voice.

She frowned at him, arms crossed over her chest.

"I need to speak with you," she said, and turned on her heel to walk to the library.

Garrett had no choice but to follow her, though he was very confused. Once inside the library, Claire closed the door with a soft click and whirled around to spear him with a glare.

"I've been hearing all over town that Mena is a joke," she hissed, jabbing him in the chest with an accusing finger. "You have to set people right. Everyone is laughing about her and saying that her father trapped you for his ugly daughter."

"Why are you mad at me?" he demanded, trying to fend her off as she continued to attack him. "I was accosted earlier by Bronnington at the club, and he knows better now."

Claire's hand dropped to her side, her face clearing.

"Oh, well good. I am so upset for Mena. It's unfair that she is treated this way, though I suppose it's not surprising."

"Why do you say that?" he asked.

Claire shifted, looking unsure.

"Well…she is not the usual sort of wife a duke would select."

Garrett crossed his arms, one brow raised in warning.

"I love Mena, you know that. I just mean that the ton are ruthless and will exploit any perceived weakness. I'm relieved you told Bronnington off. What did you say about the rumor regarding her father?"

Garrett sighed.

"The rumor never came up, but if that is what Bronnington heard, it was utterly nonsense to think that Sir Harvey-Morton had anything to do with it. We made our own choices, and this is the result. I am quite happy with how it turned out."

Claire broke into a brilliant smile. She stepped forward to hug her brother tightly.

"Good, as am I. Mena is the best thing that has ever happened to you, brother. Don't forget that."

With that she swept off back to her bed, presumably, leaving Garrett slightly overwhelmed by the truth of Claire's words. Mena was the best thing in his life, and he was very happy with his marriage. With a bemused grin he made his way back to the warmth of his wife's company.

* * *

In the morning, Mena descended the stairs on her way to the breakfast room. Garrett had left early that morning for a meeting, so she had lain in bed far longer than usual. As she passed the parlor, she noticed the dowager countess seated alone, picking at a piece of embroidery.

"Good morning, your grace," Mena said as she stepped into the room. "Have you had your breakfast yet?"

The older woman squinted up at her, leaving her work forgotten in her lap.

"Oh yes, I was up long ago," she said, waving a gnarled hand in the air. "Come sit, my dear. Call for some tea, if you like. But there is something I need to discuss with you."

Mena nodded, prickling concern racing down her spine. She forced herself to push that feeling aside and rang for a tray to be sent in before taking a seat across from the dowager.

"What is it?" she asked, keeping her hands relaxed in her lap, though she itched to start smoothing them over the fabric of her skirts.

"There is a rumor circulating through society. That my son only married you to poke fun at the ton," the dowager duchess said, lips pursed as she looked down her elegant nose at Mena.

The floor seemed to drop out from under her. Was this true? Was everything they had built a marriage upon false? Was everyone, including Garrett, laughing at Mena behind her back? The room seemed to spin, and Mena dug her fingers into the plush velvet of the settee for support. The dowager frowned as she took in Mena's reaction, and Mena wanted to scream in frustration.

"I'm sorry, your grace?" Mena said with a slight shake of her head.

"My son, he was using you, dear. He always was difficult, and saw an opportunity to both annoy me and make a mockery of the ton."

She sipped at her overly sugary tea, her lips remained pursed as though she had sucked a lemon.

"Who is saying this awful thing?" she whispered.

"I do not know who started it." She spat the word out like it was poison. "But believe me, it will be in the society papers soon enough. Many tongues are wagging. Claire told me early this morning that Bronnington is the loudest voice."

Mena took a shuddering breath. "What should I do?" she asked weakly.

The dowager sighed, and set aside her embroidery. She speared Mena with a look.

"I know my son. He can be an idiot, but he is not cruel. Talk with him about it."

Mena stared at the tea tray and the rapidly cooling brown liquid in her cup. The tidy cucumber sandwiches sat ignored on their dainty china plate.

"There is something else," the dowager said, her voice hesitant.

Mena looked up, alert. What else could there be?

"There is a rumor that your father somehow orchestrated your marriage. That he was the cause of you being caught together."

Her sharp eyes watched Mena's reaction. Mena felt her blood pounding through her veins, and almost wished she could faint. She licked her dry lips.

"It is true," she confessed, her voice barely a whisper. "My father told me when he came to town."

The dowager inclined her head, expression carefully concealed.

"That is a problem," she said.

Mena stared down at her hands. What was happening? Her marriage was finally settling into something...genuine, she'd thought. She was a fool. She had thought it was love, but instead it was simply a new ruse designed to humiliate her. It was boarding school all over again. When would she learn not to hope, not to expect more? She wasn't cut out to deal with the ton, nor did she want to.

Fuck this life. She'd never sought this out, and she wouldn't play along anymore. Mena jumped to her feet and dipped into a shallow curtsy.

"I find myself in need of a rest. Please excuse me, your grace," she managed through clenched teeth, and strode from the room.

Her jaw ached from the tightness she held herself with; needing to hold herself together lest she burst apart.

Mena lifted her skirts, clenching the silk in her shaking hands, and ran up the stairs (faster than a duchess was allowed). Upon arriving at her rooms, she slammed the door behind her and leaned back against the door, breaths coming fast and shallow. What was she going to do?

The puppy lay on Mena's bed, and she went over and snuggled up to the fluffy little creature, burying her face in its warmth. She should never have left home. Physical pleasure wasn't worth this kind of existential pain and humiliation. It was time to go back where she belonged. She had been wrong to think that this was love. She had been naive and caught up in lust, that's all.

Mena resolved to send a telegram to Clem and take the train back to Buckinghamshire. She picked up the puppy, holding it close against her body, and rang for a maid. If Mena was good at one thing, it was running away. She was an expert at that.

"Please pack my things. I'll be leaving on the 5 o'clock train with a small bag, and the rest can be sent along," she instructed her maid, Lydia, once she'd arrived.

"Where to, your grace?" Lydia asked, bewildered.

Mena considered this. Where should she go? Surely her father wouldn't send her away, but neither did she want to face him after his role in this debacle. Thalia and Clem would both take her in, but Thalia was newly married and deserved time alone with her husband. Besides, Mena couldn't stomach seeing a happy couple just now, especially one so sickeningly in love. So, Clem was the winner, but first Mena would simply go to the estate. It was her home, after all.

"Buckinghamshire please, Lydia."

The butler opened the door for her, and Mena stepped out onto the front step. Rain fell at a slant though the sun still shone brightly through the gray clouds. Mena stared at the rain for a moment before resolutely pulling up her cloak hood and descending the front steps to the waiting carriage. She was going home where she belonged.

But first she had to save Lady Crane.

* * *

The carriage pulled up in front of the Crane residence, a stunning red brick manor house located in the finest section of Mayfair just beside the park. The footman handed Mena down, and she signaled for him to follow as she made her way up the front steps to rap on the door. The knocker had barely touched the lacquered wood before the door burst open and Lady Crane emerged looking frenzied.

"Oh, I'm so relieved you've come," she gushed, her eyes darting side to side in search of her husband. "My husband's plans have changed. He could be back any moment."

Fear gripped Mena's heart for a moment, stealing her breath. But this was hardly the first time she had faced down danger.

"Of course I came, but we need to move quickly," Mena said, careful to use a calm tone as she would for a frightened animal. "Do you have any bags? John here can assist you."

"Yes, only the one trunk and a carpet bag. Please, let's go straight away."

John grabbed the items, as the butler looked on. The butler made no move to stop them, although he could hardly be unaware that Lady Crane was leaving her husband. Mena stepped up to the man and handed him a bank note.

"It would be good of you to not say anything to Lord Crane until absolutely necessary," she said.

The butler took the note with a nod and shut the door firmly in her face. Mena turned and flew back down the steps to join Lady Crane in the carriage. John settled the trunk and bag, and jumped up to take his place as the carriage began to roll off. Lady Crane looked out the window, her foot tapping nervously on the floor. Mena reached over to squeeze her knee.

"Set your mind at ease, Lady Crane. You are free of him now," she said, her voice firm.

Lady Crane turned to meet her eyes, her liquid brown ones warming as she took comfort from Mena's touch. She let her hand drop down to her lap, closing the carriage curtains to shut out the city that rolled by.

"Where are we off to?" she asked with false cheer.

Mena sat back, smothering a jolt of melancholy that threatened to cause her control to slip.

"I am headed back to Buckinghamshire for a visit," she answered. "There is a safe house for you in the city. A place no one will come looking for you. From there you can decide what to do. You will have options."

Mena finished with tenacity, wanting Lady Crane to know and fully comprehend what it meant to be free, with no man to play her master. This was no less than all women deserved, but especially someone who had never had a taste of that freedom to begin with. Mena was struck with gladness that she was able to help another, but also a heavy curtain of despair settled down upon her.

Lady Crane nodded, and tried to sit still as they made their way to Bethnal Greene where the network of suffragettes living in London had a townhouse, one of many, where women could stay for a while with access to information and resources to plan their futures. Employment could be secured, travel fare, housing, schools for children, as well as basic necessities. Women were not saved from their prisons only to be cast into the streets; they needed support.

"This is not a wealthy part of town, Lady Crane. But here you can hide away for a little while. You will be very safe, I promise you. Write to me if you ever need me," she said when they arrived at the nondescript townhouse tucked away behind the flower sellers and lingering silk mills.

"Thank you, for everything, your grace," Lady Crane said with a slight sob.

Mena watched her go, making sure the door was opened and Lady Crane safely inside before she tapped on the ceiling for the carriage to continue on. To the train station, and back home.

Chapter

Twenty-Six

At White's, the gentlemen's club where the men of parliament met and forged the alliances that shaped England's future, Garrett sat reading the morning paper as he awaited a meeting. His mind kept circling back to thoughts of Mena, whom he had left sleeping in bed earlier that morning, and he marveled that he'd had the strength to leave.

This revelry was interrupted by the swaying, drunken form of Lord Crane, red-faced and stumbling on his unsteady feet, into the library. Garrett stood, unease sweeping through him as he tossed the paper aside.

"Good afternoon, Lord Crane."

Crane waved a servant away who had come close with glasses of champagne and straightened to address Garrett.

"Bedford, my wife is gone," he said accusingly.

"Is that so?" Garrett replied, confused. "Are you hoping for assistance in locating her? I might suggest the Metropolitan Police."

He shoved his hands into his pockets and sat back on his heels.

"Don't be an ass," Crane slashed a hand through the air.

"My apologies, Crane. What did you just call me? I must have heard wrong," Garrett's laugh had an edge, warning Lord Crane to step carefully.

But the other man was too drunk to be reasonable, and he stuck a long finger in Garrett's face, expression contorted with rage.

"I know your *wife*," he spat the word, "knows where she is. I want her back now," he roared.

An attendant rushed over then and advised Crane to calm himself or he would be asked to leave the club. Crane scowled at the man but adopted a less aggressive stance.

"I just want my wife," he whined, suddenly looking defeated.

There was no sympathy in Garrett's heart for him though, knowing what Mena had told him about Crane's behavior. Garrett was enjoying watching the man suffer.

"Even if I knew where your wife was, Crane, I certainly wouldn't be telling you about it," he said with false calm. "Now I suggest you head home and sleep this off before you do something you might regret."

Crane's eyes sharpened at that, and he drew himself up, his mouth opening to speak. But the attendant cleared his throat loudly, distracting Crane for a moment. He appeared to reconsider, and turned to leave, but not before tossing a priggish look Garrett's way.

Garrett watched him leave, then sat back down. He wanted to go home immediately and check on Mena, feeling unsettled that someone so vitriolic was focusing on her as a target for his wrath. But his meeting was set to begin any moment, and Garrett looked up to see Viscount Darlington heading his way, his jaw set in the way that meant he was ready for an argument. Garrett forced aside the worry that pulled at his mind. Mena was fine, and he would prove that to himself as soon as Darlington was done with his presentation.

"Crane lost his fucking mind, huh?" Lord Beckwith said, after suddenly materializing to Garrett's left.

The surprise was entirely unwelcome. Garrett reached for his drink, tossing back the contents to avoid answering Beckwith's question.

"We need to talk, Bedford," Beckwith said, turning serious.

Garrett took his time setting the glass back down, then crossed his arms to consider the other man.

"About what? I didn't think things were so bad between us that you would stoop to spreading gossip about me."

Beckwith blinked at him, mouth agape. Apparently the accusation was a surprise to the man. Garrett shook his head, unsure how to read that response. He had expected some kind of an argument, at least.

"I have had no part in gossip at all, Bedford. I have been trying to warn you, ever since you came to town. There are some vicious tongues, and some of those are attached to unpleasant people who wish your wife ill. I am not one of them."

The earnestness in Beckwith's voice gave Garrett pause. But history told him not to trust the other man, who had never shown an ounce of concern for Garrett before.

"Why not? You were there in Buckinghamshire and have had plenty of time to share memories with those very same sharp-tongued aristocrats you now warn me of."

"Believe me or not, the result is still the same. I regret not being able to warn you sooner," Beckwith said, exasperation in his tone.

The man's sincere expression had finally cracked, revealing his annoyance. He blew out a breath, raising his eyes to the ceiling as though searching for patience up there in the plasterwork.

"It is not me who has been spreading rumors, Bedford. I've never been against your union. In fact, I set out to warn you about the gossip following you to London. The night of the opera, I was trying to help. If you hadn't brushed me off, things might have turned out differently."

"Impossible."

But Garrett was losing his certainty. Perhaps Beckwith was telling the truth. The man had no real motive to destroy Garrett's marriage and reputation, other than ancient schoolyard frustrations. Was Garrett's memory about those youthful years even accurate? He couldn't be sure.

"When I heard Crane was looking for his wife—who had lived beneath the man's boot until you came to town with your new duchess—I put things together and attempted to intervene. Obviously, I failed."

"We were never friends," Garrett reminded him, perhaps a touch too harshly.

Beckwith's lips lifted at the corners, a bare curve of the hard flesh, but no humor touched his eyes.

"Whatever I may have done in the past to contribute to any misunderstanding, it was not my intention. I've always respected you."

"You always seem to turn up at the right time to see me embarrass myself," Garrett replied, watching the other man's reaction carefully for any signs of deceit.

"My movements are not entirely unfettered," Beckwith said. "I have to do what I'm told."

Garrett snorted, a humorless noise of disbelief. "That's a silly excuse, my lord. Aren't you turning thirty this year?"

There was a pause, and then, "You know how fathers can be," Beckwith said softly.

He was avoiding Garrett's eyes, and shifted in a show of discomfort. Ah, now Garrett understood. He considered Beckwith with new eyes.

"Yours too?" he asked.

The other man nodded slowly, a pained expression crossing his face before disappearing again. He had had years of practice keeping his features smoothly arrogant.

"I knew what was going on the moment I heard the details from the Countess of Crenshaw. Your wife's father is a meddler, and I was worried for you both."

"So, you weren't spreading the rumors?"

Beckwith met his eyes then, deadly serious. "No. I wouldn't do that."

Garrett believed him. Even as a youth Beckwith had never been one to engage in subterfuge, preferring instead to face situations head on with honest clarity. Garrett appreciated that and wondered why they had never been friends before now.

Perhaps it was maturity that brought one around to the true values that mattered in life—things that are harder to appreciate when a person is young and focused on selfish independence. At least now the two men were finally forging the relationship they ought to have had all these years.

"Well, I appreciate that, even if it's too late to change anything now."

"What do you mean?"

Garrett shook his head with a smile playing on his lips. "It's too late to change anything now because I'm quite taken with my wife, and I don't give a shit what the ton has to say about it."

"I'm happy for you," Beckwith said, sounding sincere.

"So, what now?"

The men considered each other, wary and unsure in this new truce.

"I need to go home," Garrett replied, rubbing a hand over his face.

$* * *$

Later, Garrett walked up the front steps to his house, eager to see Mena. But upon entering he was struck with a strange sense of loss, the house felt more empty somehow. Silence settled into the wooden bones stretching into the dull afternoon light as the clock on the wall chimed the hour and dust motes floated in the sideways light beams. He stood there absorbing this in a sort of emotionless stupor—frozen in time. What did it mean?

The butler had closed the door behind him and stood waiting for Garrett to speak. Garrett cleared his throat and turned to him.

"Is the duchess at home?" he asked, amazed at how normal his voice sounded to his own ears as his body vibrated with alarm.

"Her grace left this morning," the butler answered.

"Did she say when she would be back?"

The butler blinked at him.

"No, your grace. Though perhaps Lydia would know, as she helped her grace pack earlier."

"Pack," Garrett repeated, his mind refusing to comprehend that word.

"Yes, your grace," the butler said. "Is there anything else, your grace?"

Garrett shook his head, unable to form words just yet. His first impulse was to rush to the sideboard and slam down a drink, or several, but he stopped himself. He didn't want to get plastered, he wanted to find his wife. Instantly annoyed by the echo of Crane's words, Garrett paused to rake his hands through his hair.

No need to panic, there must be some explanation for what was going on. He needed to ask the maid, Lydia, and it would somehow make sense. He made his way down the hall to the library, where he rang for a footman.

"Please tell Lydia I would like to speak with her," Garrett told John once he arrived.

When the diminutive maid cautiously entered the room, Garrett invited her to sit down. He took a chair opposite, and tried to smile and set her at ease, but he was unable to conjure much of one.

"Lydia, I was looking for her grace, but she doesn't appear to be at home. Did you help her pack?"

The young woman looked terrified, the color bleached from her already pale cheeks.

"Y-y-yes, your grace," she stammered. "Her grace wanted to bring as much as she could take with her to Buckinghamshire. Then she took a carriage to the station. But she didn't tell me anything about it, I swear to you."

"Thank you, that's fine. I just didn't know she was planning a trip," Garrett replied, and settled back in his chair as desolation overtook him.

Lydia looked sympathetic but offered no further explanation. Garrett bid her leave, and let his head fall back against the top of his chair. Why would Mena leave? What had happened?

"You look dejected, Bedford," the dowager said, her dry voice jolting Garrett from his despair.

"I am, mother," he replied, his eyes tracking her advancement across the room until she settled herself into the vacated chair.

"Your wife spoke to me this morning before she left."

Garrett's head snapped up. He straightened in his seat.

"What did she say?" he asked, close to pleading.

His mother considered him for a moment, before sighing.

"We spoke of the rampant rumors in town," her sharp eyes boring into him. "She was distressed to hear about the tale of her father trapping you. It is most unbecoming, I must say."

"Mother," Garrett warned. "It's just a rumor. We don't need to give it more weight than it deserves."

"Well, that's just it, my dear boy. It might not be complete fabrication, given her reaction to the news of it. And you have no reason to understand this, but a woman's place in society is not easy, not even for those of us born and bred for it. Your wife needs support all around her to live this life."

Garrett considered that, shocked that his mother was giving him wise advice. It was unlike her to involve herself in anything remotely emotional regarding her children, let alone to have taken the side of a country girl, who might have elevated her station by duplicitous means, against the judgment of the ton itself. The dowager stared back at him, seemingly completely at ease with her sudden change of engagement with her offspring.

"What should I do?" Garrett ventured, allowing his vulnerability to reach out for a connection with her.

The dowager laughed softly.

"My dear, I love you, but you can be quite obtuse. Go to her and tell her you love her. Philomena will be fine, as long as you two are facing these obstacles together. That girl thinks she can weather every storm on her own, much like someone else I know." She nodded to him with a twinkle in her eye.

Garrett gaped at her, but recovered quickly.

"Thank you, mother," he said as he stood, and leaned over to press a kiss on her cheek.

The dowager waved him off, and Garrett almost ran to the hall and to the front door. The butler looked mildly surprised, but asked what his grace needed.

"Call for a carriage, please. I'm off to catch a train," Garrett replied, shrugging back into his coat and gloves.

* * *

Mena sat in the blue parlor before a modest fire she had seen to herself. There was something comforting about stacking the coals just so in the hearth, and watching the flames build in intensity as they were set ablaze. She settled into her chair, lost in the dancing flames behind the grate.

It was strange how much the manor house felt like a home now, when so recently she had thought it could never be one. Even though she had only spent a short time there between the wedding and being whisked off to London, she had grown quite fond of it. Sitting there in the parlor, the manor was a safe haven for Mena. She was mistress of this domain. The thought was cheering, though it wasn't enough to erase the shadows plaguing her mind. Her marriage might very well be over before it had really begun. The loss was immense.

It was early evening now, and she should eat something, as she had missed lunch. But she couldn't muster an appetite yet. Perhaps she would take a bath first and eat in her room. But her room here was filled with memories.

The steady sound of footsteps drew closer until the air in the room changed, an electricity crackling in the air. She could feel his presence. She hated the flare of hope that kindled in her heart.

"You came for me, then?" she asked without turning, her gaze still focused on the fire.

Garrett came around the side of her chair and looked down at her for a moment before he spoke.

"Yes, I wanted to know what was wrong. Why did you just leave like that, without a word?" he said calmly.

Mena sighed and sat up to look at him.

"I couldn't…I just needed to get out of there," she answered honestly.

Garrett went to sit, close enough to touch her, but kept his distance. He studied her face, hunting for understanding. Mena wanted to cry in agony, but she was numb.

"I know it isn't easy to tell someone else not to panic, but I want you to trust me. You can come and tell me anything, Mena."

Mena took a breath, willing herself not to fall apart.

"Your mother told me that people believe my father tricked you into marrying me," she said.

"Yes, and it's ridiculous. Just ignore it," Garrett exclaimed.

Mena frowned. That wasn't possible, nor would it solve anything. She could not simply tell herself to ignore such deliberate meanness from people she was forced to spend time with socially. But it was also not a fabrication at all.

"My father told me," she whispered, her voice almost breaking. "He confessed to sending in the countess to interrupt us. He suspected us and set about to catch us in the act."

Garrett absorbed this in silence for a moment.

"But we were still alone together, doing exactly what he suspected of us," he pointed out, reasonably.

Mena was caught up short.

"Yes, but…" she struggled to find something else to say. "I'm just not sure I can go back there…to face them all with such vile things being said everywhere I go."

"It will take some time to settle in, please give it a chance."

"Let us do both of us a favor and end this charade. I am not a duchess, and you do not want a wife. Maybe this was a mistake," she said miserably, her shoulders curling inward.

Garrett's face fell, the hope draining from his expression.

"What?" he choked out.

"I think it's best if we both accept this marriage isn't going to work, and part ways now, before we grow to resent each other," Mena said, forcing the words out.

"I'm not so eager to give up on us," Garrett replied, somewhat lamely.

Mena stared at him, chest rising and falling with her rapid breaths.

"I don't know that love is enough."

Her words landed between them. Silence ensued.

"I know this life, this marriage, isn't what you wanted. But you are a fighter, a natural champion of causes you believe in. The world needs you, wielding this power. And I think you want it. Don't be afraid. Our love will be a foundation, not a prison. Please fight for us; believe in us."

"But you were concerned before, about the nature of my advocacy. Will you not eventually come to harbor a grudge against me?"

Garrett shook his head, coming to her with hands spread wide.

"No. I am in awe of your drive to better the world. Believe me when I say that the rumors about us are not true, Mena. While I enjoyed the way marrying you nettled the elite, our marriage wasn't a lark or a joke. I wanted you." He took a breath. "I still do."

Mena didn't want his words to affect her, but rebellious emotions coiled their way through her, inspiring a warmth to bloom in her chest. She scowled.

"I agreed to marry you because you persuaded me, and I wanted to trust you. I don't know how that trust can be repaired."

"Please come home with me and we can figure this out together."

"Garrett, there is nowhere to go from here. I cannot breathe from the humiliation of this," she held his gaze.

"I never wanted any hurt to come to you, Mena," he said.

"I know," she replied.

Garrett stared at her, jaw set. His impassive expression revealed nothing of his thoughts. Only the white of his knuckles as he clenched his hands on the back of the chair belied his emotional state. Mena forced herself not to squirm or look away. She was strong enough to stand up for herself. She had done it before and survived, and she would survive again.

"Fine," Garrett bit out.

And he swept from the room, closing the door firmly behind him. Mena sagged, feeling the tension in her shoulders dissolve into an ache. She rolled her head, trying to stretch, as though the answer to her conflicted emotions lay in her muscles.

It surprised her that Garrett would give up. It seemed out of character. But then again, she hardly knew him at all.

Chapter
Twenty-Seven

Mena clutched the wiggling puppy in her arms, taking immense consolation in its warmth and vivacity. Thalia's sitting room was growing less chaotic as new curtains and rugs had been delivered, and several pieces of art had been changed out on the far wall.

Despite the cheerful company and delicious cakes, Mena was suffering from what could only be described as heartsickness. The squeezing pain in her chest was distracting, circling her thoughts back to Garrett over and over, though she tried desperately to put him out of her mind.

"Passion is overrated anyway," she grumbled. "I want more. I want love."

Thalia gave her a sympathetic look, causing Mena to want to curl into a ball and escape the pity in her friend's eyes.

"I think a good marriage should have both passion and love. The passion is best when the relationship is built on trust and communication," Thalia replied as she refilled her teacup.

Mena released a frustrated sigh and let the puppy jump down to the floor to snuffle for crumbs.

"Well, that's not a good sign for my marriage then, is it? We have no trust, and we don't communicate."

She crossed her arms over her chest, hugging herself for comfort. Thalia frowned.

"You deserve everything, Mena. It isn't too much to ask for those values from your relationship," she murmured softly.

"How does one create trust though?"

"It must be earned."

Mena sighed and reached for a chocolate hazelnut cake slice. She bit into it, but the crumb left her mouth dry, and she could barely taste it over her misery. Thalia considered her for a moment.

"Do you believe the duke cares for you? And has your best interest in mind?" she asked.

Mena barely hesitated before nodding.

"And do you believe he would keep your confidence?"

"Yes, I do," Mena replied slowly.

Thalia smiled, looking satisfied, and sipped her tea.

"But that doesn't prove anything," Mena protested.

"Yes, it does! You trust him. And I would bet you that he feels the same way about you," Thalia replied.

Mena tilted her head in thought, considering this. Was that true?

"Even if there was trust…how can I live the life of a duchess? It is hopeless," she said, feeling pressure behind her tired eyes as tears threatened.

"With trust, anything is possible. You were not alone in London, with the dowager and Lady Claire. And if you love him, having Garrett by your side would eventually drown out any negativity around you. But if not…you could work out a schedule that pleases you both. Marriages also require compromise," Thalia stated, confident in her assessment.

"I don't know…" Mena whispered. "I feel so…conflicted."

"Don't feel that you need to decide right now, just think on it," Thalia responded with her usual assuredness.

Mena nodded, wishing she could feel so calm and confident about…anything. But she felt pulled in multiple directions, and uncertain about where she would land. The future had never seemed so bleak before, not since her mother had died. It felt risky to gamble everything on a marriage that could leave her heartbroken in the end. Though she already felt heartbroken now…

***

Once back at the estate, Mena was surprised to see a carriage waiting in the drive. The Bedford crest was blazened on the doors, and Mena's heart skipped a beat as hope flared within her. Had he come back? Would he beg her to return with him?

She flew up the steps and inside, only to discover the dowager awaiting her in the parlor. The older woman looked up as Mena entered, and she patted the seat beside her on the settee.

"Come sit by me, my dear girl," she said.

Mena cautiously came closer and sank down beside the dowager. She reached up to remove her small hat, decorated with a spray of false roses, and set it aside.

"Good afternoon, your grace. I did not expect a visit today, or else I would have been home to receive you."

The dowager waved this away with one gnarled hand.

"It doesn't matter, Philomena. I did not mind the rest after the journey getting here. I came to speak with you about my son."

Mena swallowed past the lump in her throat. Uncertainty made her nervous, not knowing what to expect, but she forced herself to stay calm and listen. The dowager took a breath and began to speak in a voice lost in memory.

"I was always told that a woman's value was her body, and that is all. She should not expect to have a voice, and should be grateful for what she is given. A woman's place is to suffer, according to my own mother."

Mena's heart ached and she reached out to grasp the dowager's hand, giving it a comforting squeeze. The older woman looked down at their joined hands, as though surprised by the gesture, but did not pull away.

"Once Claire was born...that way of life became much harder to endure," she continued.

Mena nodded and dared to put her arm around the dowager's shoulder for comfort. To her surprise, the dowager leaned into the embrace like butter melting on warm toast. She soaked up the physical touch with the swiftness of someone starved for affection. For someone so privileged, so powerful, to be in such naked need...it was disarming.

Mena knew how it was to live this life that society demanded, but she couldn't do it any longer, and her mother's death had released her entirely from the pressure to conform. No one had given the dowager that ability.

"So I began to travel. It was a way to escape the ton and all their rules…but it meant leaving my children behind with their father. And I don't believe they will ever truly forgive me for that. If I have one regret, it is that loss of connection with my children."

Mena wiped a tear from her cheek.

"I understand. My life was all planned out for me—a marriage to someone who would elevate my family, and a long list of rules to abide by. I was never meant to be a whole person," she said.

The dowager nodded.

"Garrett came to see you," she stated, but in her eyes was a question.

"Yes, he did," Mena nodded, feeling the urge to avoid the dowager's probing gaze.

"I suppose the argument remains unresolved?"

"It isn't exactly an argument, your grace," she clarified.

"How would you characterize it then?"

Mena sighed.

"Our marriage is not built on trust and honesty," she said. "Once rumors started circulating and all the secrets were revealed, the marriage was over."

The dowager pinched her lips together, nostrils flared.

"Over," she repeated. "Perhaps my efforts will be wasted, but yet I will try."

"I hoped you weren't merely here to try and change my mind. Would you like some refreshment?"

Mena stood to ring for a footman. Within seconds one appeared—Thomas, the second footman.

"Please bring us tea and some of those marvelous scones Merideth made this morning, thank you."

Then she retook her seat.

"You have a way of dealing with the servants," the dowager commented.

"I treat them like fellow human beings, you mean."

The dowager broke into a smile.

"Truly, you are quite something, my dear. Now, what do you plan to do? What do you want for yourself?"

Mena looked up at the ceiling, studying the intricate plaster work.

"I don't know," she replied honestly.

"Close your eyes. Imagine yourself in five years. What do you see?"

Mena obliged, though it felt silly as she let her eyes drift closed. She settled herself, leaning back against the back of the settee, shuffling pictures in her mind until she settled on one that made her heart skip a beat.

It was a scene of home, family, love. And Garrett was a part of it. Perhaps reconciliation was possible. Her eyes flew open with a gasp. The dowager gave her a knowing smile.

"You deserve happiness, my dear. That is all I wish for my children, and like it or not, you are also my child now," she said softly.

Mena's heart squeezed in her chest. Without thinking, she threw her arms around the dowager, and pulled her into a tight embrace.

"Thank you," she whispered.

Twenty-Eight

In an effort to maintain some semblance of sanity, Mena returned to the orphanage to keep herself busy. If she could find a path back to routine, maybe she could organize her thoughts and emotions and finally know what to do.

Part of her wished to return to London and seek out Garrett for reconciliation. Another part of her wanted to wait for him to come back and beg her to return to him. And yet another part of her was afraid to risk her heart, preferring the known emptiness of her former life to the unknown future.

Distracted by her thoughts, Mena turned the corner and found herself bumping into a lanky boy, who promptly crashed to the floor sending marbles rolling in all directions.

"I'm so sorry, let me help you," she rushed to say as she pulled the boy to his feet and started gathering up the marbles.

"I'm fine, don't worry yourself ma'am," he said, bending to scoop several glass orbs into the leather pouch he held.

Mena cursed as she tripped over several marbles but managed to stay upright. With her hands full she turned to the boy to place them in the pouch, and recognized the youth.

"Bart! What are you doing here?"

He looked up at her, surprised.

"Every week I come for my lessons, ma'am. The duke doesn't want me to neglect my studies even though I'm a stable boy now."

He puffed his chest out proudly as he spoke, and Mena felt warmth bloom in her chest.

"Well, I heartily approve of that. You are capable of anything you set your mind to, Bart. Never forget that," she said with a smile.

He considered her for a moment, a question clearly begging to be asked. Finally, he did, unable to contain his curiosity.

"Everyone is saying that you married the duke. Is that true? Are you a duchess?"

Mena hesitated, not wanting to make a false statement, but her marriage was legally binding, after all.

"Yes, it is true, I am now the duchess of Bedford," she replied, feeling the title settle over her in a new way; it felt…right.

"The duke is a bang-up gentleman. He will give you jewels to wear," Bart declared with a firm nod.

Mena smothered a laugh. Of course that is what a child would focus on, the spoils.

"That is an excellent point," Mena replied carefully. "My life has changed so much."

Bart nodded sagely.

"I understand. Change is hard," he said seriously, somehow intuiting what Mena struggled with. "But I would like to have you about the estate. I miss seeing you."

Mena's heart gave a squeeze.

"May I give you a hug, Bart?" she asked, bending down to his level.

"Yes, of course," the boy answered, and eagerly leaned into her embrace.

Mena held the boy tightly. No longer did his clothes hang on his scrawny frame, with dark circles under his eyes. Now he felt so strong and healthy in her arms, with the same buzzing energy as always, but contained in a way that showed his growing maturity. He was blossoming, and change was a part of that.

From the mouths of babes, Mena thought to herself.

"I shall see you at the estate then, Bart. Pay close attention to your lessons now," she said, and the boy nodded enthusiastically.

"Oh, I always do," he said, and tipped his hat like a tiny gentleman before skipping off down the hall to his destination.

Mena watched him go, feeling unsettled. The boy's adoration toward Garrett made her impulse to go to him all the stronger. Why was she fighting that instinct so?

"Your Grace, there is someone at the door for you," a maid called, causing Mena to jump in surprise.

"I'll be right there," she said, turning to make her way to the front door of the orphanage.

Who would come to see her here? She shouldn't have been surprised to find her own husband waiting there, clutching a riotous bouquet of hothouse blooms, but she was suffused with shock at the sight of him.

Garrett was a handsome man at all times, but at this moment, perhaps from missing him the past few days, he shone like a sun, beckoning Mena to throw herself into the blaze. She was a moth dragged toward the light, despite her fears.

"Good morning, your grace," she stammered, suddenly self-conscious that the maid was still there, observing.

Garrett smiled faintly, his eyes glued to her, full of uncertainty.

"I apologize if you needed more time, but I found I couldn't stay away," he said.

The smooth rumble of his voice sent a shiver down her spine. She had missed him terribly. She craved his touch. Yet she held herself back.

"I am…happy to see you," she said carefully, finding it the most honest thing she could say at that moment.

Garrett's eyes filled with hope, and he held out the flowers he was clutching.

"These are for you. They reminded me of your spirit, wild and beautiful."

Mena looked down at the blooms, so many different ones making a unique and arresting combination. She was moved to think he saw something in them that brought her to mind. He had been missing her too. Suddenly she wished to bridge the gulf between them, though unsure how to make the first step. But she didn't get a chance to, for Garrett suddenly lowered himself down to the stone landing, his back to the bustling village street.

Right there in front of the town, the powerful Duke of Bedford dropped to his knees in supplication to beg for his wife's return.

"I want you back, not because I want to control you or change you into something different, but because I love you. I love who you are, your passions, your advocacy, your dreams and desires. I wish to be a part of your life, and share in those dreams.

Please, Philomena, I beg you to come home to me and let me love you."

His bright blue eyes held all the sincerity she could have wished for, and seeing a powerful man brought to his knees was certainly a powerful feeling—and she had caused this. But still she hesitated. People rushed past them, headed to work or on errands, but a small crowd was gathering to observe the display. Mena shifted uncomfortably.

"Let's talk about this inside, please," she urged, and tugged Garrett's hand until he stood.

He flashed a lopsided grin—an instinct he simply couldn't quell. Mena pressed her lips together, but resisted rolling her eyes as she pulled her estranged husband inside. The heavy door slapped closed behind them, giving them an illusion of privacy. She crossed her arms, chin tipped up as she regarded Garrett.

"Now, what were you saying?" she asked, tapping her foot impatiently.

He looked less certain now, but cleared his throat to begin his speech once again.

"Philomena, I love you. I love the life we were building together before you left. The way you annoyed the ton was amusing. You don't care a whit for what they think and their idiotic traditions. I admire that, and it makes me feel stronger by being beside you. As I set out to convince you to marry me, I fell in love with you. I love you, your spirit, everything about you. You are the woman of my fucking dreams. Please, please, come home with me. I'll do anything to make it better."

Mena stared at him, this man who was her husband, trying to resist his words and the way they snuck into her heart, warming and growing in strength. She should have fortified herself against him, but honestly how was she supposed to stop herself from loving him? Garrett was all things good and kind and genuine.

She loved him.

"If I do come home, will you ask me to live in London?"

"God no! Don't ever feel obligated to do anything you do not wish to do. I want you in my life in any way I can have you," he said, clutching her hand to his chest so she could feel his hammering heartbeat.

Mena broke into a slow smile.

"I love you too, Garrett. Let's go home," she said.

Garrett's look of relief was so intense it almost buckled her knees, but he was there in an instant, scooping her up into his arms for a kiss so penetrating and sinful she forgot they weren't truly alone.

"Excuse me, but would you mind doing that in the privacy of your own home?" a woman's voice called from down the hall.

Mena and Garrett broke apart, turning to see who it was. Mrs. Farningham, the orphanage's headmistress, was watching them with her arms crossed over her ample chest. She tried to look severe, but Mena knew the older woman was holding back a laugh.

"So sorry, ma'am, we'll make ourselves scarce," Garrett replied, and carried Mena toward the door.

"Will I see you tomorrow, Mena?" Mrs. Farningham called.

Mena looked at Garrett.

"No, I think not," she replied, eliciting a delighted squeal as Garrett pushed open the door to carry her out to his awaiting carriage.

"Good!" Mrs. Farningham called, but her voice was lost in the noise of the busy street.

Garrett settled Mena into the carriage before climbing in after her, and pulled her back into his embrace. He wasn't going to let her go again, Mena realized, and that was good because she never wanted to let him go again either.

The end.

Epilogue

"So what's next for you?" Mena asked.

Clem sighed, brushing a rogue lock of hair from her brow. She turned away from the papers littering her desk to meet Mena's eyes. She had shadows beneath her lovely green eyes, and her glossy black curls desperately needed a brush. Mena worried over her friend, knowing that Clem was often in danger of neglecting her health in her crusade to change the world.

"Well, I cannot stop this new factory from coming. The local politicians are set on it. They call it progress," Clem said with a roll of her eyes. "I will pivot to targeting the women who will be hired. They deserve some empowerment in this."

Mena nodded.

"I will help in any way I can. Please let me know what to do."

Clem smiled and hugged her friend tightly.

"I love that about you. I will send word when I have a task for you. But for now, go home and rest."

"Will you come for dinner tomorrow?" Mena asked, feeling the need to make sure her friend got a decent meal in.

Clem smiled, clearly understanding the direction of her friend's thoughts.

"Yes, I promise. Go now! Let me get back to work," she laughed, flapping her hands at Mena to go, as though she were a bird to scare off.

Mena allowed Clem to force her out, though no one could stop her from worrying. It was what she did best. But the carriage ride home was soothing, the rocking and swaying almost putting her to sleep, like a baby in a cradle.

At the estate house, she startled when the carriage rolled to a stop, and practically jumped out in her eagerness to see her husband. The footman rushed to catch her by the elbow and assist her up the icy steps, lest she stumble on them and injure herself. Ridiculous really, but Mena was grateful for the assistance. She removed her gloves and hat as the door opened to reveal Mosley.

"Good afternoon, your grace," he said with a bow as she entered.

"Good afternoon, Mosley. Is my husband in the library?"

"Yes, your grace."

Mena swept down the hall, giddy to see her husband.

Garrett looked up from his desk, which was strewn with papers, a twinkle in his eye. He tossed his head slightly, causing a lock of golden hair to fall across his brow, obscuring one eye. Mena shook her head, forcing herself not to melt on the spot. She had important news to impart. Seduction would have to wait for later.

"How was your visit with Clementine?" Garrett asked, pushing himself back in his chair.

"Very good," Mena said, coming around the desk to settle into the edge of it. "I also had an appointment with Dr. Blakely."

He was instantly alert, one hand coming up to rest on her thigh. Mena could feel the burn of his heat through her layers of silk and cotton. She shivered with delight.

"Is that so? Everything all right?" he asked.

Mena smiled, like a cat eyeing a mouse.

"Yes, it is wonderful," she paused, drawing out the anticipation of the moment. "We are going to be parents soon."

Garrett's jaw fell.

"Really?" he asked, eyes wide.

"Yes," Mena said, smiling brightly.

Garrett lifted her easily, pulling her onto his lap. He held her face in his large hands and kissed her breathless.

"That is wonderful news," he said against her lips.

Mena nodded, a sob caught in her throat. It was the best news, and for once she was certain of the future. With this man by her side, and their child—a product of their love bond—the future was very bright indeed.

About the Author

Rebeccah Wilson is a life-long lover of romance, having picked up the habit in middle school and never looked back. When she isn't writing, Rebeccah can be found in the garden or walking the numerous nature trails near her house. She lives in Massachusetts with her husband, three children, an ill-behaved dog, a bearded dragon, and far too many chickens.

www.ingramcontent.com/pod-product-compliance
Lightning Source LLC
Chambersburg PA
CBHW032032310726

48972CB00002B/641